Horsés Heroes

Jonkers

Grosvenor House
Publishing Limited

This book is published by
Grosvenor House Publishing Ltd
Link House
140 The Broadway, Tolworth, Surrey, KT6 7HT.
www.grosvenorhousepublishing.co.uk

This book is a work of fiction. Any resemblance to
people or events, past or present, is purely coincidental.

A CIP record for this book
is available from the British Library

ISBN 978-1-83615-236-1

Also by Jonkers:

Jimpy

Jimpy 2 (Chaos and Cat-astrophe)

Terry Scope's Telescope

I'm So Ugly (and other poems)

The Legend of Lommie

Dedicated to

Janette (Mrs Jonkers)
And Luke

My Mum
My Dad

With Love

Horsé Marinio

'The Gaffer'

PRE-MATCH WARM-UP

David and Goliath. Tom and Jerry. Jack The Giant Killer. Tweety Pie and Sylvester. Don't we just love it when the underdog comes out on top? Of course we do! We're British (although I'm actually Portuguese). It's what we do. You will have heard about our amazing underdog story in the papers, on the T.V and on social media. In fact, pretty much everywhere. You will know about the big games, the players, the victories and defeats. You will know my name, Horsé (Hor-say) Marinio. But now, for the first time, you get the full story direct from those who were actually involved; who were actually there. Players, coaches, physios, the people who really were – 'Horsés Heroes'. The full story, right from the 'Horsé's mouth (so to speak).

FIRST HALF
(HOW IT ALL STARTED)

CHAPTER 1 –
PEP TALK

So how did it all start? What was the spark that lit the fuse? Well, believe it or not, it all started in a field in Hampshire on a blistering hot day in early Summer. I was sitting back in my wooden deckchair, wide-brimmed sunhat perched on my head, a pair of Ray Bans protecting my eyes from the dazzling glare of the sun, a cold beer in my right front hoof, relaxing as the local team battled with bat and ball against a nearby village. Only the sound of leather on willow, murmured voices and birds singing their melodic little tunes, drifted into my ears. As quintessentially English as you could possibly get. There were only two or three overs left until tea (cucumber sandwiches and slices of Victoria Sponge washed down with a cold glass of squash or a good old-fashioned cuppa). And that's when I first saw him (or heard him to be precise).

"Good game?" That was the first thing that he said to me, something that he would repeat many times in the future, usually without the question mark. I'd heard him before I'd seen him because I'd actually nodded off. I woke with a slight start and looked around. Just to the left of me, curled up in a huge coil on the scorched, brown grass, lay one of the biggest snakes I'd ever seen in my life.

"Oh...er.. yes, not bad," I stuttered. "Young chap in at no.3 got a good half century."

"Lovely day."

"Yes. Perfect cricket weather."

We continued in this vein, simple small talk, up until the tea break. Then he said the words; the words that were to set the whole thing in motion. He said, "Of course, I'm really a football nut but I don't mind watching a bit of the old bat on ball." 'A football nut.' That was it. Three simple words. We got talking about football, our favourite teams, our opinions on players, about the leagues, promotion, relegation, VAR. We hardly noticed the players coming back onto the pitch after the break. We just talked and talked about 'The Beautiful Game.'

The match ended and the local side had won by fifty-three runs. The players sportingly shook hands and good-naturedly left the pitch, heading for the ancient, whitewashed, wooden pavilion. It was only then that I realised that I hadn't even introduced myself to my newly acquired friend. "I'm Horsé, Horsé Marinio." I held out my hoof to him without thinking that he hadn't actually got any limbs to shake with. Instead, he nodded. "I'm Pep, Pep Anaconda, it's been nice chatting to you."

Two weeks later, we bumped into each other. Once again, we were at the cricket ground. This time however, and typical of our wonderful 'British summers', the skies were filled with ash-grey clouds and there was a hint of dampness in the air. It was also about ten degrees cooler than the previous week and I'd resorted to wearing a jumper and a thin raincoat. When Pep turned up, he too was wearing a plastic cover over the top half of his body and a yellow sou'wester on his head.

"Morning Pep, bit different to last time, hey?"

"Just a bit. Typical, unpredictable British weather. Is it still on?"

"It is at the moment, but the forecast doesn't look great. Feels like it's drizzling a bit harder already."

Sure enough, within minutes the drizzle had turned to torrential rain, with lightning and thunder bursting through the clouds. By then though, I'd just about made it to the pavilion and sheltered beneath the covered balcony. Pep took longer as he slithered across the grass and heaved his long, thick frame up the balcony steps. We both sat down on the green, moss-stained bench and stared out towards the pitch. The rain was lashing down and large puddles were already forming on the wicket and on parts of the outfield. The clouds were now a solid mass of black that plunged the day into night.

"Do you think the umpires will be coming out with their light meters?" Pep quipped with a broad grin on his face.

"I don't reckon they could even see their light meters in this gloom, let alone read them," I quipped back. "I think we can safely say, Rain Stops Play!"

"Fancy a quick pint down the Pig and Trumpet? (Foalchester's only pub)."

I looked at my watch, made a bit of a face as though I was seriously weighing up the suggestion before finally saying those well-worn words, "Ok then, just a quick one!" To be honest reader, there was no possible way that I was going to go home as the wife and I had just started re-decorating the lounge, so I was grateful for any excuse not to go home yet (not sure I should really be admitting this but hopefully my wife won't read it). Love you honey!

Three pints of beer, and an hour and a half later, we were still sat on the comfy sofa, as the rain continued to thump hard against the windows. On the widescreen TV behind the bar, they were showing highlights of the previous season's Premier League. Just like our previous meeting, we started to analyse the play, give our opinions, and share thoughts and ideas. Amazingly, we seemed to be in almost total agreement with how we thought the game should be played and systems that suited particular teams. As the highlights finished, our talk moved on to discussing any local teams. There were a few sides locally, but only in Sunday league football. There were no local sides playing in a Saturday League.

Another beer later and Pep made a suggestion that was to prove the start of something truly amazing. He said, "What about... What about...me and you starting up a team?"

I assumed he was joking, or the beer was talking, but he looked deadly serious. "I'm serious," he said (I told you he looked serious!). "If we were to go and watch some of the Sunday sides and put an ad in the local paper... Could be fun."

CHAPTER 2 –
GOING FOR THE DOUBLE

Where to start? Early June already and the new season would start at the beginning of September. There were training sessions and friendlies to organise before that. Oh, and one more *quite* important thing – some players!! Oh, wait a minute – and somewhere to play. Oh, wait another minute – registering to a league. Oh, and one more thing… Well, you get the gist, there was a heck of a lot to do if this mad scheme was even going to get started.

I knew that a couple of the young lads who played for the local cricket team also played football. I also knew that they were more 'cricketers who played football' than 'footballers who played cricket.' They played in one of the lower divisions of the local Sunday league. I thought though, that it might be worth having a chat with them and see if they knew any local players that might be interested in playing in a higher league on Saturdays. We met up in a coffee shop on the high street. As soon as I mentioned our idea, both the boys immediately suggested the same two players – Rhinodinio and Rhinaldo – twin brother rhinos who played for a team called Hornshead Common Rovers. They told us that both were really gifted players and that they were playing way below their abilities. Apparently, they had both had trials to play for professional clubs when they were in their late teens. They were only 23 years old now. This was sounding extremely promising. But…

"So how come they're just playing Sunday League football?" I asked. The lads just looked at each other and smiled. I didn't really like the smiles. There was something behind those smiles, something that may just take the shine off things.

"Well," one of the lads began, "they weren't about for a few years."

"Not about?" I said nervously.

"For a couple of years. Serving under His Majesty's pleasure."

I'd heard the phrase before but at that moment I just couldn't quite understand what they meant. Had they been in the British Army? Were they on the King's private staff? Caterers? (They had mentioned 'serving').

"Under His Majesty's pleasure?"

"Yeah, you know, put away for a couple of years. In chokey, doing stir, doing porridge. Prison."

"Prison?" My enthusiasm and optimism plummeted as quickly as my hopes had been raised earlier. I remained silent for a few moments and mulled over what I'd just been told. Ok. Prison. Prison. Mmm... Ah, prison maybe, but what for? It may have been something relatively harmless like fraud, or embezzlement, or they'd got caught up in a brawl somewhere. Wrong place, wrong time perhaps.

"What for?"

"Armed robbery."

"Ahhh." So much for the relatively harmless crime!

"It wasn't a real gun they used."

Did that make it any better? I thought to myself. I don't suppose the people that they were waving the gun at would have seen it that way when they found out. "Oh, that's alright then, so it was just a very convincing replica gun. Bless them, the little rascals!" No! They would have been terrified!

"They're not bad lads really," the other boy chipped in. "They just did something stupid. They'd become addicted to gambling and had got themselves into debt with some very unpleasant people. Don't tell them that I said this," he whispered, looking around the room first, "but they're just not the brightest people in the world. I've heard that they've stopped the gambling since they were released and have settled down a bit. One of them, Rhinaldo I think, is married with a kid now."

"Ummm...?"

"Why don't you go and have a chat with them? You'll see, they're decent lads really."

I talked to Pep about the rhino twins and we both agreed that we should at least go and meet them. Then we could make up our own minds about whether they were the type of player that we wanted as part of our team. We'd contacted them and agreed to meet them during a lunchbreak at their workplace. They worked together as part of a team carrying out highway maintenance. Today they were working fairly locally, just eight miles away in Snakeford. I drove, as Pep, being a snake, had no arms or legs and had never learnt to drive. By the time the fully adapted 'Snake' vehicles had been produced, Pep was already late middle-aged and hadn't really felt the need to learn. He was the owner of a car-crushing business in Bone Town and had done very well for himself. He had plenty of money to use taxis or pay friends or colleagues to take him about. Today he had just climbed into the car and curled up in a massive coil on the back seat.

We arrived a little earlier than we'd arranged, and the lads were still working. They appeared to be the only two rhinos in the team, so they were very easy to spot. One was sitting in the cab behind the controls of a massive yellow digger. With headphones on his head, he looked the picture of concentration as he scooped up the debris in the giant bucket. His brother (and we had no idea who was who at the moment) was using his horn to dig deeper into the long trough along the road. They were big lads. Yes, they were rhinos, they were obviously going to be big, but these two looked even bigger than your average rhino. They also looked identical (and no, rhinos certainly do not all look the same!)

I parked up a little way down the road and we waited. Soon, the digging stopped, and the digger driver clambered out of the cab. I climbed out of the car and gestured with a wave of my hoof. I got their attention, and they ambled down towards us on their back legs, lunch bags and Thermos flasks by their sides. After brief introductions we walked to a large park across the road. Pep and I sat on one of the benches and the two rhinos sat down on the dusty, dry ground. The rhino that had been in the cab was Rhinaldo and the one using his horn for digging was Rhinodinio. The only slight difference between them was that Rhinodinio had ground away a bit of his horn, presumably from years of digging.

"So," I began, "as you know from speaking to us on the phone, Pep and I are planning to create a Saturday football team in the local area, hopefully in the Southern National league. We've been told that you are two of the best players in the area."

"Right," said Rhinaldo, in an extraordinarily deep voice.

"We were just wondering if you might be interested. Obviously, we haven't seen you play yet but from what we hear..."

"Yeah, we can both play a bit, although we ain't exactly fully fit at the moment." He looked across at his brother and grinned. "Put on a few pounds, ain't we bruv?" He gave a gruff little laugh. Rhinodinio smiled and nodded. It seemed that he was the quiet one of the two. "Who else ya got?"

"No one yet. You're the first ones we've approached, but we have had quite a few replies from our adverts. We want to assure you that we are serious about this venture. We know it isn't going to be easy, it's not a bad standard of football."

"You'll need to be fully committed," Pep added. "There'll be training twice a week, and we'll expect you to be reliable and willing to work hard. I'm happy to offer expenses and a few quid for matches." That was the first I'd heard of that, but I knew that most teams in this league paid their players. The rhinos looked at each other, Rhinaldo raised an eyebrow slightly. Rhinodinio gave a slight nod.

"Yeah, we're in. But we'll wanna see what players yer get in first."

"Great. Now..." I took a breath before continuing, "Sorry to have to mention this, but I understand that you got into a bit of trouble a while ago."

"Yeah."

"Well...can we trust you? Is... is all that behind you now?" I stammered. They were big lads!

"Yeah, we was just being idiots, we ain't done nuffink since. Weren't great being stuck in a cage wor it Dinio?" Rhinodinio shook his head. "Straight as a die now mate, steady job, got a little nipper now an' all!"

"Great to hear it," I said, relieved. I must admit that I'd been very nervous about mentioning their criminal past. As I've already said – more than once – THEY WERE BIG LADS!

Rhinaldo

Weight: Oi watch it! (Approximately 3,500 Kg but will try to lose a bit!)
Speed: 45 MPH when fully fit – currently nearer 35 MPH.
Height: 1.8 M

Job: Highway Maintenance Operative – (Digging up roads!)
Age: 3 minutes younger than my brother
Where were you born?: Hornchurch

Favourite position: Lying down on the sofa
Favourite film: HORNey I Shrunk the Kids
Favourite actor: Rhino Neal

Favourite joke: Why don't you see rhinos hiding in trees? Because they're very good at it!

Rhinodinio

Weight: About the same as my brother (but a little bit less!) Approximately 3499 Kg.
Speed: 46 MPH when fully fit – currently nearer 36 MPH (a bit quicker than my brother!)
Height: Slightly taller than my brother (approximately 1.81M)

Job: Highway Maintenance Operative – (Digging up roads!)
Age: 3 minutes older than my brother.
Where were you born?: Hornchurch.
Can you play a musical instrument?: Yes, the Horn!
Favourite position: Sitting on my brother when he's lying on the sofa.

Favourite Joke: Why is a rhino's skin so wrinkly? They're very hard to iron!

CHAPTER 3 –
JIM PAN ZEE

One of our biggest worries was to find a decent keeper. We'd asked around locally, but nobody really seemed to fit the bill. Then we got an e-mailed response to our ad from a young lad called Jim Pan Zee. He'd only just moved into the area but had previously been in goal for one of the best non-league sides in the country, Gibbondale Town. This sounded promising. We swiftly set up a meeting at the head office of Pep's car-crushing business. When I arrived, Pep was already there in the office, leaning back on a swish, leather swivel chair. On the visible top half of his body, he was wearing a pin-striped tube over a white cotton top with a small collar. Attached to the top was a navy blue, elasticated tie. I had to hand it to him, he really looked the business. Perhaps he'd over done it a bit, but he certainly fitted the role of Chairman of our new club.

Jim Pan Zee arrived a few minutes early and we asked him inside. First impressions were that he appeared a bit short and not hugely athletic for a chimp. But, if he'd been playing at Gibbondale, he must be half decent.

"Good morning Jim, thanks for coming. I'm Horsé, Horsé Marinio, and this is Pep, Pep Anaconda. Can we get you anything to eat or drink before we begin?"

"Oh, that'd be lovely. Thanks."

"Coffee, biscuits, a piece of swiss roll?"

"Erm, a milkshake and a banana would be great."

"Right, certainly, what flavour shake?"

"Erm, banana if you've got it, please."

Pep talked into a small device clipped to his collar and asked for a banana shake and a banana to be brought to them.

"Shouldn't be too long. My assistant is just going to pop into town and get them. Unfortunately, we don't keep bananas here as my entire workforce is made up of various varieties of snakes, apart from my assistant Kevin, he's a kangaroo. Anyway, can you just give us a little insight into why you might want to come and join our club?"

"Well, Mr Marinio..."

"Horsé, please."

"Horsé. I've heard what you're trying to do, forming a new club and all and it sounds really exciting. I've had to move into the area because of my job, but it was really tough leaving Gibbondale. I'd been playing with them for five years, starting in the reserves, then making my way into the first team. I still wanted to play, whatever, but I thought I'd probably have to play in a local Sunday League side or a five-a-side team. Then I saw your advert."

"Sounds great. What are your strengths as a keeper do you think?"

"Well, I dare say that when you saw me you thought I was a bit short and not particularly athletic for a chimp..."

"No, not at all," I lied.

"Well, despite my lack of height, one of my strengths is that I'm good in the air, coming for corners and so on. I've got a good leap, long arms and, if I may say so, a safe pair of hands. I'm stronger and braver than I look too."

"You look strong enough to me," I lied again.

Pep, who hadn't actually said a word yet, finally spoke.

"I'm certainly liking what I'm hearing young man. Obviously, we'll need to see you in action, but if you do sign for us, we can only offer a fairly small amount of money. If you don't mind me asking, did you get paid to play for Gibbondale?"

"Yeah, but peanuts to be honest."

"Well, we can't offer much here either I'm afraid."

"That's fine, I'm happy enough with the peanuts."

"Oh, sorry," Pep said, smiling, "I didn't realise that you actually meant 'peanuts'. I'm sure that we can manage that. Maybe even a couple of bags a week and a bunch of bananas for a clean sheet. Anyway, we can talk more about that if and when we offer you a contract. We're hoping to set up our first training session next Saturday if you're available."

"Perfect."

"We'll be practicing at the Mongoose Lane ground, at 11.00 a.m."

"I'll be there."

Outside, in the hall, there was a loud thumping and banging noise, followed by a knock at the half-open door. Kevin (the kangaroo assistant) had arrived back and his head suddenly appeared around the edge of the door.

"Ah, Kevin," Pep said, "come in."

Kevin hopped inside, bashing his head against the lampshade and knocking a small bin over with his tail. We all stared at him. He was absolutely covered in thick, yellow goo. It ran all down his white shirt and down onto his shorts, dribbling right down to his enormous feet. The milk shake had been much more than 'shaken'.

"Sorry boss, the lid came off the shake when I was jumping my way back. I've got the banana," he said holding it up pathetically in his left paw.

"That's fine Kevin, don't worry. Go and clean yourself up."

Kevin left, leaving myself, Pep and Jim. There was silence for a moment, then Pep suddenly burst out laughing. Jim and I quickly joined in. We'd both been almost bursting inside trying not to laugh. Poor young Kevin, it was a bit mean to laugh but, well...It wasn't everyday you saw a banana milk-shake-covered kangaroo!

Jim ate the banana and the meeting continued for another five or so minutes. We were all pleased with the way it had gone.

"Thanks for coming Jim, it's been great meeting you," I said.

I shook his hand and Pep nodded to him. Perhaps, just perhaps, we'd got ourselves the keeper we'd been looking for. Only time would tell.

Jim Pan Zee

Weight: 40 Kg
Height: 35cm (short for a chimp, but I'm very agile!)
Speed: 25 MPH

Favourite singers/bands:
Banana Miskouri (Greek singer),
Bananarama,
The Arctic Monkeys
Superhero: Banana Man

Favourite food:
Bananas
Favourite drink:
Banana milk shake
Favourite dessert:
Banana splits
Favourite flavour crisps: Banana
Favourite T.V programme:
The Banana Splits

Favourite Joke:
What kind of key opens a banana?
A Monkey!

CHAPTER 4 –
MARCUS AND THE GIANT

By the time the day of the first training session had arrived, we'd heard from many more potential players. We hadn't had time to meet anyone else, but we were optimistic about the turn out. We'd also made it clear that it was a completely open trial, so we were hoping for a few surprises to turn up.

The Mongoose Lane ground had previously been used by a Sunday League side but hadn't been used for a couple of years. It was a full-sized pitch with plenty of free space around it. There was also a decent-sized building housing the changing rooms and showers, and a small stand on opposite sides of the halfway line with dugouts closer to the pitch. The pitch itself was fenced off with short metal railings. If the club was to really take off, there was plenty of room to extend or rebuild the stand or even (and we were really dreaming here) build a sizeable stadium. Even at this stage, we were thinking big. We hadn't even had a training session yet, or got a squad of players, but Pep's enthusiasm was catching. Thinking back, it sounds crazy, but at the time it just seemed ... well...'right'.

Pep and I had arrived at the ground at 10.30 a.m. We'd also brought along Sid Silverback, a fitness coach from the nearby Champford Rugby Club. He was another of Pep's contacts (he seemed to have contacts everywhere, for just about anything). Sid was, as you might expect from a four-hundred-pound gorilla; muscular, imposing, solid, with a no-nonsense approach to training. (I've got to be honest here, he scared the hell out of me!).

The first player to arrive was Jim Pan Zee. He was already dressed in his goalkeeping kit – bright yellow jersey, yellow shorts, yellow socks, and yellow boots. He'd even got his gloves on already and we couldn't help noticing that the fingers of the gloves looked very much like bananas, yellow with dotted patches of brown. Now, most chimps are keen on bananas, but this guy just seemed obsessed with them. You might say, he was bananas about bananas! (Sorry about that awful joke, I'm sure the editor will take it out!) He came and joined us as we waited for others to arrive.

Next to arrive, together, was a cheetah (Chi Tah) and a lion (Lionelli). Then the rhino twins turned up. They walked over to us.

"Alright boss?" Rhinaldo greeted me. Boss? I liked it.

"Hi boys. Thanks for coming."

"No probs. We've brought a mate along. Hope that's ok."

I looked around but couldn't see anyone. I actually looked around the side of them to see if their 'mate' was somehow hidden behind them. Then Rhinaldo pointed to his left with his horn. He was pointing downwards. I looked. There was a rat. A large rat, but a rat all the same. Now, I've got nothing against rats, indeed some of my best friends are rats, but they weren't exactly well known for being footballers. For one thing, they were rather small.

"This is Marcus," Rhinaldo announced, "Marcus Ratface."

I walked forward and shook his paw. "Nice to meet you, Marcus." At the time I didn't know just how important this moment would prove to be.

More arrived. There was a pig (Terry Trotter), a Dromedary (one humped) camel (Camelino), an elephant (Eric Elephantona), a crane (Harry Crane), a flamingo (simply called Flamingo), a zebra (Zebrado), a cow (Moo Salah) and a Scottish Terrier called Kenny Dogleash. There were a number of others as well, probably over thirty altogether including a few surprising trialists such as a snail and a grass snake. Again, I'm not being deliberately prejudice but I couldn't help noticing that obviously the snake didn't have any limbs at all

Marcus Ratface

Weight: 4.2 Kg
Speed: 9 MPH
Height: 9cm

Job/Education:
College, studying catering

Favourite T.V show:
Rats of the Day

Favourite Film:
Ratatouille

Favourite Singer:
Rat King Cole,
Ratalie Imbruglia

Favourite Food:
Anything and
everything!

Fears: The Pied Piper

Favourite Joke:
What do you call a rat
with a wooden leg?
A pie-rat!

and the snail, as well as being an extremely slow mover, also only had one 'foot' and that was the sticky underside that he used to propel himself along. Still, they all deserved a fair chance. We wanted to be inclusive.

The cones had been set up, the speed and agility training ladders had been laid down, and we were all set to start the warm-up and stretches. Then HE walked into view, walking slowly and serenely towards us, legs like stilts, a neck stretching up almost as far as the eye could see, and finally a proud, distinguished head seemingly nudging the clouds. I know what you're thinking, 'of course he's tall, he's a giraffe', but believe me, this guy was like a giraffe with an extension built on. Everyone, even Sid Silverback, stopped what they were doing as the colossal beast came across the field. Then I recognised him, or at least I thought I did. If I wasn't mistaken, this was Jack Longneck, former professional footballer for Longleat Town of League 1.

"Good morning," he articulated in a smooth, velvety voice. He looked down at me. "Ah, I believe you must be Mr Marinio." He held up his front right foot and we tapped hooves.

"Please, call me Horsé."

"Certainly, Mr Horsé. My name is Jack, Jack Longneck, you may possibly have heard of me, I used to play for Longleat Town." I'd been right, I could hardly believe it. He'd been a top League 1 player, and it was widely believed that he could have got into any team in the Premier League and possibly into the National team. As it was, he'd shown great loyalty to Longleat and had played for them for almost eight years, since he was a young lad. He'd retired from professional football at the end of the previous season, still being voted as Player's Player of the Year and Supporter's Player of the year. He'd wanted to go out whilst still near the top of his game.

"Yes, of course I've heard of you."

"Marvellous. I was reading in the local newspaper that you were trying to put together a non-league Saturday side and it sounded interesting. May I join in?"

Jack Longneck

Weight: 1,200 Kg
Speed: 30 mph
Height: Very, very, very tall.
(Approximately 5.7m)

Dislikes: Low Roofs
Strengths: Good in the air

If you weren't a footballer, what would you be?
Still very, very, very tall.

Favourite film: Giraffic Park
Fears: Heights
Job: Ex-professional Footballer
Nickname: Shorty

FUN FACT: On his debut, he ran out of the tunnel, whacked his head very hard, felt concussed and had to miss the game!

FAVOURITE JOKE:
Some giraffes can grow up to 18 feet - but most only have four!

"Er, yes... of course. You..." I stuttered. Jack Longneck. Jack Longneck! I could barely believe it.

With Sid barking orders, the players were soon being put through their paces. Pep and I stayed at the edge of the pitch, watching to see who stood out. During the fitness training, there was one player that really stood out, and interestingly enough it was Rhinaldo and Rhinodinio's rat friend, Marcus. He may not have been very big compared to most of the others, but he was lightning quick and showed great agility. If he could actually deal with the size of a football and had a useful technique, he could be a great asset to the team.

This was soon tested as Sid introduced some balls into the session. They began with simple dribbling between cones. Marcus fairly flew around the cones, mostly using his nose to keep the ball under control. When he needed to pass the ball to the next player in his line, he stood up on his back legs and passed the ball firmly and accurately with his right, back leg. For a small lad, he seemed to have little problem with the weight of the leather ball. I looked at Pep and he looked at me.

"Think we may have one there," he said, with a knowing smile on his face. "Looks a bit useful."

I merely nodded in agreement.

As the session continued, and a match was set up, I started to make a few notes, both of my thoughts and those of Pep.

Jack Longneck – Strong, calm, very comfortable on the ball. Great in the air. Class!

Jim Pan Zee – Clean handling, brave, agile – lack of height doesn't seem to be a problem.

Rhinaldo – Strong, surprisingly quick, good on the ball. Lacks a bit of fitness. Enormous potential.

Rhinodinio – Skilful for a big lad, hard to knock off the ball. Also lacking a bit of fitness.

Chi Tah – Very quick, needs to work on end product but lots of potential. Seems fully fit.

Camelino – Strong lad, lacks a bit of pace but seems to read the game well.

Eric Elephantona – Another strong lad, good feet, sees a pass well – big presence.

Lionelli – Skilful player, works hard and strong in the tackle. Good all-round footballer.

Terry Trotter – Quite a twinkle toes (or twinkle trotters!) Great ball control. Not the quickest and definitely not fully fit. Could be useful but would need to train hard and probably lose a few pounds, or stones!

Harry Crane – Natural right wing-back, good pace and likes to get forward. Neat and tidy on the ball.

Flamingo – Natural left wing-back? Possibly. Possible left winger. Good pace and a bit of flair.

Kenny Dogleash – Busy player with bags of energy, great movement. Scored a couple in the session – natural predator in the box? Could be a key player.

Moo Salah – Gets up and down the pitch well, keeps hold of the ball well. A bit one-paced but may be a useful target man.

Zebrado – Energy to burn! Full of tricks. Exciting prospect. Might be a bit of a luxury player.

Marcus Ratface – Pace to burn, agility, ball control – looks the part.

Gazzer Grassnake and Jonjo Shellby – Unfortunately, found it all too much. Out of their depth. Still not quite sure why they've chosen football as their sport. Nice couple of lads though. Keen as mustard! It would be nice to get them involved in the club in another way.

For a first session it had been very positive. Some clearly needed to work on their fitness, especially the Rhino twins and Terry Trotter, but overall, it was a very promising start. If they all signed, we'd have a squad of fifteen players. We'd need a few more but it all seemed to be coming together surprisingly well.

We later found out that Gazzer and Jonjo hadn't actually meant to come to the training session, they'd just been going for a walk (or slither) together across the field and had somehow got caught up in it all! What a pair! Now we'd *have* to keep them with the club!

CHAPTER 5 –
FRIENDLIES

After three weeks of training, we'd managed to fix up a friendly with one of the local Sunday League sides, Kertsey Social. Our kit had arrived in the week: blue shorts, blue socks, and blue and white striped tops. We'd also all but settled on our official name. As we were based in the small town of Foalchester, we'd tried Foalchester Town, Foalchester Rovers, Foalchester Social and AFC Foalchester. In the end we'd thought about how we needed to come together as a team and as a town, so we settled on Foalchester United. The pitch had now been cut and properly marked out, the goals had been put up and we'd applied to the league for registration. Meanwhile, Pep had managed to get some workers in to make sure that the changing rooms were cleaned and re-decorated, the showers were fully up and running and the ground, as a whole, was up to standard (he had contacts in the building trade! Of course he did!). I sometimes wondered what he'd say if I was thinking of flying to the moon, probably that he 'knew some bloke...' Anyway, things were really moving.

We set up in a 3-5-2 formation.

1. Jim Pan Zee – Goalkeeper
2. Camelino – Central Defender (Right)
3. Jack Longneck – Central Defender (Centre)
4. Terry Trotter – Central Defender (Left)
5. Rhinaldo – Central Midfield
6. Lionelli – Central Midfield

   7. Harry Crane – Right Wingback
   8. Chi Tah – Central Midfield
   9. Kenny Dogleash – Striker
 10. Marcus Ratface – Striker
 11. Flamingo – Left Wingback

Subs: Rhinodinio, Eric Elephantona, Moo Salah, Zebrado

We gave Jack Longneck the captaincy and he won the toss. We were to kick off. The first player to touch the ball for the newly-formed Foalchester United was Marcus Ratface. He nudged the ball forward and Kenny Dogleash played it back to Lionelli. We were away!

We played the ball about nicely and soon created an opening for Kenny Dogleash, who crashed the ball against the post. So close. Just six or seven minutes into the game, Harry Crane flew down the wing and swung in a cross that was well defended at the expense of a corner (obviously, Harry didn't actually fly as his wings, as well as those of Flamingo, had been clipped as per F.A rules). From the resulting corner, taken by Rhinaldo, Jack Longneck easily outjumped everybody and calmly nodded the ball downwards and into the back of the net. 1 – 0 to Foalchester. Within fifteen minutes it was 2 – 0, a blistering burst of speed from Chi Tah had seen him one-on-one with the keeper who came out well to block the initial shot, but Kenny Dogleash had been there to tap in the rebound. The opposition were working hard but there was a clear gap in terms of quality. Two became three after the half hour mark, Terry Trotter blasting a thunderbolt from just outside the area. The keeper had no chance. It remained 3 – 0 at half time but the pressure from left to right had been almost constant. Jim Pan Zee had barely had a touch (in fact at one point he'd rooted through his boot bag and pulled out a banana that he'd then proceeded to eat).

Pep and I had a chat with the boys, praising them for the way they'd kept the ball and totally dominated the game.

We made it clear that there would be much trickier opposition to come, but that for a first competitive game they'd gelled together really well. The attitude and commitment had also been good. We swapped Rhinaldo for Rhinodinio, Zebrado for Chi Tah and Eric Elephantona for Camelino. We wanted to make sure that all the players had a run out. We intended to bring the three withdrawn players back on later in the second half.

Despite the changes made, the match continued in similar fashion with our team having the vast majority of possession. Marcus Ratface was next on the scoresheet with a deft little finish over the on-rushing keeper. Rhinodinio soon made his mark with a well taken free kick, curling the ball into the bottom corner of the net. Five became six with possibly the best goal of the game, a super back-hoof from Zebrado after excellent work from Lionelli. With just two minutes of normal time to go, Jim Pan Zee was finally called into action, albeit a comfortable save from a long-range shot. The match finished 6 – 0. A useful, if not overly competitive first match. They wouldn't always be this comfortable.

Our next friendly was against Cowdean Rovers, a Saturday team playing just a division below the one that we'd joined. This was going to be a tougher test. And so it proved. We started again with the 3-5-2 formation and with the same starting eleven. We saw a lot of the ball for the first fifteen to twenty minutes but had failed to create a chance on goal. Then, we got caught on the break and after a sharp exchange of passes, the ball came to their centre forward, Adam Allama. He had time to take a touch and guide the ball accurately into the bottom left corner. Despite a desperate, last-second dive by Jim Pan Zee, the ball settled in the back of the net. We'd conceded our first goal.

We continued to have more of the ball though, and we did at last manage to create a chance, or maybe more of a half chance. Chi Tah had made a great run in behind and had pulled

Kenny Dogleash

Weight: 9 Kg
Speed: 17 MPH
Height: 27 cm
Favourite food: Scotch Eggs
All-time favourite player:
John Terrier

Favourite group/singer:
Boney M, Bone Jovi, Snoop Dog
Favourite song:
Who Let the Dogs Out?

Favourite composer:
Johann Sebastian Bach
Favourite film:
Bark to the Future

Favourite joke:
How did the Scottish dog
feel when he saw the
Loch Ness Monster?

He was terrier-fied!

the ball back to Lionelli on the edge of the box. He caught it well, but it was always sailing wide of the right upright. The pressure was beginning to tell though, and next to have an effort on goal was Marcus Ratface, who created his own opportunity by jinking skilfully past two defenders. His left foot shot beat the keeper but struck the foot of the post and bounced kindly to a defender who cleared the ball back over the halfway line. At least the game seemed to be opening up and we were just missing that clinical edge and a little bit of luck. The half time whistle went with the score still 1 – 0 to Cowdean.

As in the first game, we brought on the four substitutes at half time with Lionelli, Harry Crane, Flamingo and Camelino being replaced. We let the boys re-hydrate themselves before getting them back together as a group.

"Ok boys, it's a much stiffer test today, but we've kept the ball well and we're now starting to create a few chances. Just try to work the ball a bit quicker as they're getting men behind the ball very quickly. Midfield and wingbacks, I know it's pretty warm out there, but I need you getting up to support the front men. Now, let's get out there and get straight on the front foot, if anybody tires, we can always bring the other boys back on. Let's do this! Anything to add Pep?" I asked.

"Not really, just keep it going, they're defending well and working hard, but they can't keep that intensity up for the whole ninety minutes. This is a good work-out boys, maybe just press a bit higher up the pitch. Let's put in a big 45 minutes."

The lads listened well and Jack, as captain, gave the boys plenty of encouragement. The game restarted. Cowdean kicked off and played it immediately over to the left. A big punt forward found Terry Trotter not properly set and as he tried to chest the ball down, he stumbled slightly and had the ball pinched off him by the on-rushing fox, Ian Brush. Brush cooly rounded the keeper and side-footed the ball into an empty net. It was an unfortunate individual error and was exactly what we hadn't wanted to happen so soon into the second half. Terry held his trotters up and apologised to his team. But it was now 2 – 0 to Cowdean. The only positive was we still had almost the whole of the second half to get ourselves back into the game.

It was Marcus Ratface who pulled a goal back on 50 minutes after a nice interchange with Kenny Dogleash. His shot had actually taken a slight deflection that had wrong-footed the keeper, but it would probably have gone in anyway. 2 – 1. We were firmly back in the match.

With just over an hour gone, we had really begun to get on top as, just as Pep had foreseen, the opposition players had begun to tire. They made a couple of their own substitutions, but it didn't really change the pattern of the game. Rhinaldo crashed the bar with a thunderous 30-yard drive. The keeper pulled off a fantastic save from a trademark Jack Longneck header. One of the defenders made a vital block on the line from a powerful Elephantona bullet. Surely something had to give soon. With just minutes left Chi Tah found an extra bit of energy from somewhere and burst past their left back. He dinked the ball over to the far post where Kenny Dogleash had made a gut-breaking run. With a diving header, he finally got the goal that we'd been desperately searching for. The final minutes were played out without another clear-cut chance for either team and both had to settle for a draw. Considering the 2 – 0 deficit, the boys had shown good character to come back so well. There were a lot of positives to take from this performance and it had been a much better workout. The next, and final friendly, was to be another step up in opposition as we were to play against Wolferhampton who had dropped out of League Two a couple of years ago, but still ran as a fully professional club. With training sessions on Tuesday and Thursday evenings, we needed to get ourselves fully prepared. The opening league match was just two weeks away. We were all buzzing with anticipation.

45 MINUTES UP

A MINIMUM OF 5 MINUTES
ADDITIONAL TIME TO BE PLAYED.

As this half of the book comes to a close, I'll finish with a brief summary of the final friendly, and a short mention of the club's first game in The Southern National League in one of the National newspapers.

RESULT

FOALCHESTER UNITED 2 – 1 WOLFERHAMPTON

Foalchester scorers: Rhinaldo (28mins pen), Flamingo (68mins)

Wolferhampton scorers: Moo Salah (89 mins og).

Report:

A tightly-fought game with both teams trying to play neat, attractive football. Rhinaldo opened the scoring from the penalty spot as Chi Tah had been brought down inside the box. A clear penalty. Rhinaldo cooly slotted the ball home from the spot. Foalchester then began to control the game and created several good chances. Eventually, one of these chances was taken by Flamingo with a powerful low drive into the bottom corner from about 10 yards after a defence-splitting pass by Eric Elephantona. Wolferhampton got a consolation goal in the 89th minute via an unlucky deflection off the knee of Moo Salah. A strong, solid performance from Horsés team.

Rhinaldo Spot on as Newcomers bag first win.

Newly-formed Southern National League side, Foalchester United, got off to a dream start to the season with a hard-fought 0 – 1 victory away to Hoofton Town. Rhinaldo scored from the spot in the 53rd minute to secure the win. Foalchester's manager, Horsé Marinio, said that he was "delighted."

SECOND HALF

UP FOR THE CUP!

PRE-MATCH WARM-UP

With the club now set up and the league games underway, I'm now going to focus on what really got us noticed and made our club, many of the players and myself (yes, even myself!) household names, if only for a brief time. The magic that is the Footballing Animals Cup (better known as simply, The F.A Cup), where Minnows can become Sharks, Tadpoles can become Frogs, Geckos can become Komodo Dragons and dreams can come true. This is that story!

TRANSFER NEWS!

Foalchester United have added to their squad with the signings of Ian Brush and Adam Allama, both from Cowdean Rovers for an undisclosed fee. They have also signed young goalkeeper, Albert Ross, from Saltbay Wanderers on a free transfer. All three players will be eligible for Saturday's 1st round F.A cup qualifier against Tort Vale Rangers.

Ian Brush

Weight: 6.5 Kg
Speed: 30 MPH
Height: 68cm

Position: Striker (not "sweeper" despite my name!)
Nickname: Fox in the Box, or Brushy

Favourite comedian: Basil Brush – BOOM, BOOM!
Favourite relative: Basil Brush (Cousin) BOOM, BOOM!

Favourite joke:
Why couldn't the fox join the Scouts? He was still a cub!

Adam Allama

Weight: 215 KG

Speed: 35 MPH

Height: 1.8 M

Dislikes: Spitting

Favourite song:
Llama Chameleon by
Vulture Club

Favourite singers:
Allama Morrisette,
Llama Gaga

Favourite joke:
How do Llamas wake
up in time for work?
They set their
allama clocks!

CHAPTER 6 –
THE CUP BEGINNETH!

1st Round Qualifier

The Tort Vale match was to be played at their ground, Tort Valley, around 25 miles away. Pep had purchased a sizeable coach to be used for our away games (he had a contact in Coach Tours! Of course he did!). The coach was wide and spacious enough for the whole team, including Rhinaldo and Rhinodinio, who I may have mentioned before were 'BIG LADS!' Unfortunately however, it was very difficult for Jack Longneck to get in comfortably. He'd given it a go and had managed to squeeze in, but he had to keep his head and neck down the whole time, and had felt very uncomfortable. Pep had promised him that they would get a sunroof fitted for future games, so that he could poke his head through the top, but until then, he decided to drive down in his own convertible BMW.

On the coach were; all the rest of the squad, me, Pep, Sid Silverback, Bill Badgergton (physio), Jonjo Shellby and Gazzer Grassnake (our accidental trialists) and, of course, the driver. Pep and I had asked Jonjo and Gazzer if they'd be interested in running a Supporter's Association and dealing with the media. They'd jumped at the chance (although neither of them could actually jump). Jonjo and Gazzer sat next to each other in one of the front seats of the coach, Jonjo wearing a blue and white scarf and blue baseball cap, and Gazzer had slipped on a blue and white woollen tube to match the team's main kit. The team had blue and white striped shirts, blue shorts and blue socks for home games and gold tops with black shorts and socks for away games, where their colours might clash (for once Pep didn't have a contact in sportswear, but, he did have a friend who had a contact in sportswear!)

The atmosphere was buoyant and buzzing on the bus (it was a coach really, but I just liked the alliteration!). There was plenty of good-natured banter between the players, with Rhinaldo's voice often heard above everyone else's. Lionelli sat on his own, wearing massive, bright red headphones and Ray Ban sunglasses. He'd gelled his mane and spiked it up a little, and wore a sharp, silver-grey suit. He was one seriously cool customer! Terry Trotter was telling jokes to anyone who would listen – mostly highly inappropriate! Jim Pan Zee was sat in the corner at the back of the coach, banana in mouth. Eric Elephantona took up the rest of the back seat and threatened to crush Jim every time the coach went round a bend. Eric also supplied some backing for the songs that were being sung, by blasting out trumpets on his enormous trunk.

The coach arrived a good one and a half hours before kick-off, giving the players plenty of time to get their kits on and have a proper warm-up and a few training drills. Sid Silverback led the warm-up and drills, whilst Jim Pan Zee and Albert Ross worked by themselves, taking it in turns to work each other through a set of goalkeeping drills. The opposition were at the other end of the pitch also working through their pre-match routines.

Kick-off time was fast approaching, and I brought the whole team together for a giant huddle. With a few words of encouragement, and a reminder of what I expected from them, I set them off, confident in a positive result. Jack, who'd arrived just a few minutes after the coach, won the toss and elected to kick-off. I'd kept the same team that had played the previous week and continued with the 3-5-2 formation.

The match began. The first real action came in the seventh minute when Lionelli was adjudged to have handled the ball just outside the area. The resulting free kick was firmly struck and on target but at a good height for Jim Pan Zee to make a comfortable save. The next action took place at the other end of the pitch with Kenny Dogleash making a bit of room for himself in the box, and clipping a snap-shot towards goal, narrowly missing the left-hand post. Foalchester were having a lot of possession and building up patiently. A good save by the Vale keeper kept out a fine, curling effort from Rhinaldo on the half-hour mark. The pressure continued but the score remained 0 – 0 at half time.

The boys took in some liquid and were offered halves of oranges. Jim Pan Zee had a couple of these and then pulled out a banana from his glove bag. I then got their attention, and we had a chat about the first half and what had gone well and what we needed to do to turn possession into goals. Following suggestions, a few little tweaks were made. We felt that the wing backs, Crane, and Flamingo, needed to get forward more and take a few more risks. Jack, as captain, made a few encouraging remarks and told the players that all they really needed to do was move the play a bit quicker so that Vale couldn't so easily get men behind the ball.

The referee called us over and the second half began. Neither side had made any substitutions. Just five minutes into the second half there was a scare for Foalchester. The lone Vale striker had managed to get through one-on-one with the keeper and neatly clipped the ball over the body of the on-rushing Jim Pan Zee. The ball nestled into the back of the net and the player began to celebrate but the linesman's flag was up. Offside. It was tight though, and it was a wake-up call for the team who seemed to raise their game as a result.

Nimble footwork from Terry Trotter on the edge of the box, gave him the chance to shoot. He caught it well, but it was too close to the keeper. The keeper dived down to his right and got both hands behind the ball, unfortunately for him though, the ball rebounded off his gloves and Kenny Dogleash showed his predatory instincts to nip in and nudge the ball over the line. 1 – 0 to Foalchester, 65 minutes on the clock. Within three minutes of the re-start it was 2 – 0. Lionelli won the ball in midfield and had slipped a slide-rule pass through to Marcus Ratface who made no mistake with a clinical finish past the helpless Vale keeper. On 75 minutes I decided to make a few changes, bringing on Zebrado, Rhinodinio and two of our new signings, Ian Brush, and Adam Allama.

With his first touch, Brush made it 3 – 0 with a neat finish from 5 yards after clever work from Harry Crane. I brought the rest of the substitutes on for the last 10 or so minutes, including a goalkeeping change, with Albert Ross replacing Jim Pan Zee. Ross though was pretty much a spectator as we continued to retain possession well and saw the game out with ease. A comfortable victory, a chance to give everyone a run-out and no injuries. Around 100 Foalchester fans had travelled up to cheer on the lads and they'd all gone home very happy. It couldn't really have gone much better. We were in the hat for the next round.

Gazzer Grassnake & Jonjo Shellby
PODCAST

GG: Good evening and welcome to the Foalchester United Podcast. My name's Gazzer Grassnake, GG, and this is my sidekick, Jonjo Shellby, JS.

JS: Hello

GG: Firstly, what a great win against Tort Vale. The boys really turned it on in the second half to secure their place in the second round. The draw is taking place while we are on air, and we hope to have details of the next round before the end of the show.

J.S: Hopefully a home tie, GG.

GG: Fingers crossed!

JS: Neither of us have got fingers GG, but I know what you mean.

Albert Ross

Weight: 9Kg
Height: 1.2m
Speed (Flying): Up to 79 MPH
Speed (Walking): Much slower

If you weren't a goalkeeper, where would you like to play?:
Probably on the wing!
Favourite bands: Wings, Noel Gallagher's High Flying Birds
Favourite song: Albatross by Beakwood Mac
Favourite actress: Kate Wingslet
Favourite Joke: What's grey and white and travels at over 600MPH? An albatross on an aeroplane!

GG: Eyes crossed then!!

JS: Nice one GG. Now, onto team news. We have heard that all the players have come out of the game uninjured, and indeed the whole squad is fully fit and available for selection for next weekend's league game away to Sharlton Athletic.

GG: Horsé, the gaffer, has stated that the team are not currently looking for any new signings, but would not rule it out if the right kind of player(s) became available. He said, "I'm happy with the strength and quality of the current squad."

JS: Talking of new signings, we should mention the debuts of Ian Brush and Adam Allama. We certainly liked what we saw, didn't we GG?

GG: Well yeah, obviously it was a bit of a dream debut for Brushy, sticking the ball into the back of the net with his first touch, but I felt Adam Allama also produced a nice little cameo for the last fifteen or so minutes. First impressions suggest a couple of really good signings.

JS: Well done and keep it up lads. Obviously, the gaffer and Pep saw something in them when we played Cowdean in the pre-season friendly.

GG: Word is that they're a couple of level-headed and hard-working players too. They've fitted in well.

JS: In news away from the actual football, we must offer our congratulations to Terry Trotter who became a father for the first time last night. His wife, Sowsy, gave birth to 6 healthy piglets, 4 boys and 2 girls at around 11 o'clock last night. Mother and piglets are all said to be doing fine.

GG: Great news! Good luck Terry. With 6 little un's I think you're gonna need it!

JS: Yes, get some sleep now Terry, trust me, it'll be the last chance you're gonna get for some time!

GG: Now, the draw has just taken place and we've been informed that we have actually been drawn away from home against fellow National League South opponents Trotton Town. Trotton are currently in 3rd place in the league, three places above Foalchester and in good, early form. It looks like a tough game.

JS: Certainly not an easy one GG, but I'm sure the boys will go in with a positive mindset and hopefully do the business.

GG: Let's hope so JS. Well, that's the end of tonight's podcast, so thanks for listening and we'll be on again next week.

JS: Up the U's! Bye for now.

CHAPTER 7 –
TAKING ON TROTTON TOWN

After 3 weeks of league games (1 win and 2 draws), it was a weekend of F.A Cup qualifiers. Time to take on Trotton Town. This time we were playing on the Sunday with a 12 o'clock kick-off time. Unfortunately, this meant that Kenny Dogleash was unavailable for the match as he had a prior engagement as Best Man at his brother's wedding. Lionelli was also missing as he had sustained a nasty gash to his shin, catching it on some barbed wire as he'd jumped over a fence, pursuing an antelope who'd been involved in a fight with a gazelle. P.C Lionelli, had still managed to apprehend the antelope but not without receiving the injury. It was hoped that the injury would only put him out of action for one, or possibly two weeks. Ian Brush was brought in to replace Kenny Dogleash, Rhinodinio replaced Lionelli, and one other change saw Moo Salah come in for Camelino who started on the bench. We kept with the 3-5-2 formation that had proved quite successful so far.

On paper, the teams looked very closely matched, and so it proved. The first half was a very cagey affair with little goalmouth action. Jack Longneck came closest for us with a powerful header from a corner, but this had flown narrowly wide of the left-hand post. A long- range effort from Rhinaldo had been comfortably saved by the Trotton keeper. Trotton themselves had been limited to a couple of speculative efforts from outside the box. Neither keeper had been seriously tested and the game was finely balanced.

The second half began in the same vein, and as the clock ticked towards the hour mark, it started to look like it was either going to be a moment of brilliance or an error that was going to decide the game.

In the end though, it was neither brilliance, nor an error. Harry Crane had shown good pace down the right wing and attempted to curl in a cross. He caught it all wrong and it sliced off his right boot. Another wasted opportunity it seemed, but then the ball sailed towards goal and the Trotton keeper was a little off his line. Suddenly, he found himself frantically back-pedalling as the ball floated over his head. He stretched up and got a paw to it (the keeper was a black panther called Claudio Sharp), but the ball carried on and nestled in the back of the net. 1 – 0!

Trotton tried desperately to get back into the game, but we kept our shape well and limited them to just a couple of half-chances. As we headed into time added on, I brought on Adam Allama and Zebrado for Chi Tah and Rhinaldo. We comfortably saw out the additional 5 minutes and we'd done it. It had been tough, and not always pretty, but we'd done it! 1 – 0 and through to the third and final qualifying round.

Gazzer Grassnake & Jonjo Shellby
PODCAST

GG: Good evening and welcome to tonight's show.

JS: Good evening. Well GG, another win, through to the next round, but what did you make of Sunday's game?

GG: Well, JS, it certainly wasn't a classic, but a win's a win, especially in the cup. Obviously we had to make a few changes, but the lads that came in did a good job. I think it was just two teams, very evenly matched, not wanting to give anything away.

JS: Yes. Bottom line – we're through to the next round. Just one game away from the F.A Cup proper. Can we start to dream?

Lionelli Messie

Weight: 220 kg
Speed: 50 MPH
Height: 1.1 M
Job: Police Officer
Favourite food: Lion Bar

Favourite actors:
Lionardo Di Caprio and
Eddie Red Mane

Favourite film:
The Lion King

Favourite T.V show:
Police Interceptors
(I was on an episode once.
As a police officer, not a
criminal).

Favourite singer/band:
The Police, Lionel Ritchie

Favourite joke:
What do you call a lion with
no eyes?
A Lon!!

GG: Why not JS. You only get to dream once!

JS: What?

GG: You only get to dream once.

JS: Well, that's not true, I've had loads of dreams. You do talk some absolutely nonsensical gibberish at times!

GG: Thank you JS.

JS: That wasn't a compliment.

GG: Thank you.

JS: Anyway, back to the game. Do you think Harry meant that?

GG: (He laughs) Oh no, JS. I don't think even Harry would try to claim that. Definitely a cross, but it went in; that's all that matters at the end of the day.

JS: True. Now listeners, as you know, the draw will once again be taking place during the show, so we should be able to let you know who we get in the next round before the end.

GG: Home draw?

JS: Eyes crossed! (Neither have fingers, remember?)

GG: Now, on Sunday, JS and I were on the team coach again and we can tell you that Jim Pan Zee turned up nearly 15 minutes late. We have been informed by Pep Anaconda that Jim could give no good reason for turning up late, so has been fined by the club. In a statement, Pep said, "We have spoken to Jim and made it clear that we all need to work together in a fully professional manner and feel that, with no mitigating reason for his lateness given, the club would have to fine him. The matter has been dealt with, Jim has apologised, and we now move on."

JS: There we have it. I know that Pep won't stand for shoddiness in his business, so he's clearly bringing this, correctly in my opinion, to the football team.

GG: Absolutely true JS.

JS: News from the treatment room now. Lionelli is said to have recovered well from his shin injury and could be ready to start at the weekend. Moo Salah has suffered a mild calf strain during training and may miss Saturday's league game at home to Swingdon Town. Apart from that, Bill Badgerton informs us that there are no issues with the rest of the squad.

GG: JS, the draw had just been made. We have got a home tie this time; a home tie against Storkport County from the National League North.

JS: Not a bad draw GG. Great to be at home. Quite a journey for the Storkport team. I believe they've been struggling a bit so far this season.

GG: Yes JS, I think they're currently lying just outside the relegation zone.

JS: Big chance for us then GG.

GG: Big chance, yes, but we mustn't get complacent, they're gonna want it every bit as much as we do.

JS: I'm sure that Horsé will drum that into them!

GG: No doubt!

JS: Anyway, that's the end of this week's podcast. Just a reminder that we are playing away to Farmham on Saturday, 3 o'clock kick off. We hope to see you there.

GG: Good luck lads! Until next week – goodbye. Up the U's!

CHAPTER 8 –
JIM

This chapter is a tough one for me to write, but I feel that I must as much has already been written about this particular subject. Some of what has been written has been accurate, some quite inaccurate, and some simply made up or pure conjecture.

It was previously alluded to that Jim Pan Zee had been fined for arriving late for the coach on match day against Trotton Town. As also previously stated, there was no reason given by Jim himself. Unfortunately, after this incident, Jim's punctuality didn't improve and when he did arrive for training and matches, he didn't seem himself. He seemed preoccupied and edgy. I did have a quiet chat with him a week or two after the Trotton game, but he assured me that he was okay and that there were just a few private issues that he needed to sort out. I left it like that, but kept a close eye on him. Apart from a couple of uncharacteristic handling errors, he'd still done a good job in goal in the league matches.

Things came to a head however, when he didn't show for the Tuesday evening training session. We assumed that he was just running late again, but by the end of the session there was still no sign of him. We tried ringing his mobile and his home number but were only able to leave messages as there was no reply.

Thursday's training session started at 7 p.m. but once again there was no sign of Jim. It was becoming clear now that there was definitely something wrong. Several of the players had also tried to contact him, either by phone, e-mail, or

Facebook. No reply had come back to any of them. I decided to drop by his flat, a small, one bedroom place on the other side of Monkton. As far as I knew, he lived there alone.

When I arrived, I pressed the Intercom system, button 7. I rang again. There was no reply. There was no way in, so I was unsure what to do. Then, a young woman pushing a pram headed to the door. As she opened the main door to the flats, I slipped in. I made my way up the winding staircase until I reached the floor containing flats 5-7. I walked across to room seven and knocked. I knocked harder. Nothing. I tried to look though a small peep-hole in the door but only got a highly-blurred image of the inside. As I leant my hand against the door, I noticed that it had moved slightly. It wasn't locked. I walked in, calling out Jim's name as I went. I moved through the living room, treading over magazines, clothes, banana skins and other junk. "Jim," I called again. I thought I heard something through one of the other doors. I walked into what was actually the kitchen. That was when I saw him. Jim. He was laying down on the floor with his head propped up against one of the kitchen units. I nudged him, trying to wake him but he didn't stir. I tried again, putting my hand against his right cheek. He was clearly breathing but still didn't respond. I poured some cold water from the tap into a glass, and tipped a little on his head. He moved slightly and grunted. His eyes flickered and slowly opened.

"Urgh? Boss?" he managed to say.

I lifted the glass up to his mouth and poured a little inside. He swallowed it, so I poured a little more. Gradually he was coming round. I couldn't help noticing all of the banana skins on the floor around him. There must have been 25 to 30 discarded, empty skins, and more unopened bananas on the table. I'd seen something like this before. I knew what was wrong. Jim had a problem. Jim was a bananaholic!

As he started to come round and I'd got him to the settee, he put his head in his hands and started to cry, deep, heavy sobs. I sat beside him and put my front right leg round his shoulders, consoling him as best as I could. To see this lovely lad in such a sorry state was truly heartbreaking.

Once he'd stopped crying, and was a lot calmer, I persuaded him to go up to bed and try to get some rest. I thought it best if I stayed with him, so I told him that I would sleep on the couch for the night. He insisted that that wasn't necessary, but I didn't feel comfortable leaving him alone in the flat considering the state he'd been in.

After he'd gone through to his bedroom, I busied myself with a good clean-up of the place. I put all the banana skins into the recycling bin and had a general tidy up. The place didn't look like it had been cleaned for some time. Once I'd washed the stacks of plates, dishes, and mugs, I wiped them and went to put them away into cupboards. This is when I discovered several bags of monkey nuts. They were exactly the same brand of nuts that we'd been paying Jim, along with a bunch of bananas. The nuts had not been touched. There hardly seemed to be any other food in the house apart from more bananas. It was looking increasingly likely that Jim's diet was almost solely bananas.

Now, as a club, we have received much criticism for how we managed Jim's issue, some suggesting that we should have spotted the addiction earlier, and some even suggesting that we were in some way culpable by paying Jim in bananas. In hindsight, obviously we would not have paid Jim with bananas had we suspected that he had an issue. But, whilst we were fully aware that he certainly loved his bananas, we did not at the time realise that he was eating far too many, or that he was addicted to them.

I called Pep the following morning and explained the situation. His immediate response was one of shock and surprise, but he was quickly discussing ways in which we could help Jim. Fortunately, Pep had some contacts in the medical profession (surprise, surprise!) and he was soon able to set up a meeting with a specialist Addiction Therapist. We also decided at this stage not to release any details about Jim's problems to the local newspapers, and to keep him fully involved in training and matchdays as long as he felt able. We really wanted to keep him around the group of players and staff to keep him occupied and let him know that he was loved and supported by the club as a whole (we informed the players of the situation but asked them to keep it to themselves, at least for now).

We also decided that I should ask Jim to move in with my wife and I for a few weeks, just so that he wasn't alone in the evenings when he got back from work (he worked as a carer for elderly chimps). My children had long since moved out so there was plenty of room. He wasn't sure at first, but I managed to persuade him to stay. We were doing all we could. Now it was down to Jim.

CHAPTER 9 –
THE CUP RUNNETH OVER

The boys had been on a good run of form in the League, winning their last two games, scoring six goals, and conceding just one. By the time the Storkport game arrived, we were feeling very confident. With the Footballing Animals Cup first round proper on the horizon, the players were buzzing. Just one more victory would give them the chance of a shot at some of the Big Boys. All professional leagues entered the competition in the next round, including the Premier League. This is what the F.A Cup was all about – the dream, the magic!

There was, though, the realisation that defeat today would shatter any dreams we may be holding. There was both excitement and nervousness around the changing room as the bell rang and we readied ourselves to go through the tunnel and onto the pitch.

Jack Longneck, as always, led the team out to great applause and singing. With seats and standing we had a capacity of around 800 people and the place looked almost full. The Storkport fans (roughly 50 of them) occupied one of the stands, and the rest was packed with our fans. Numbers had been steadily rising throughout the season, but this was easily our biggest crowd so far. The local paper had sent down a photographer to capture the action and the local radio station had sent down a small team of journalists. We were slowly starting to be noticed. For a small ground, the atmosphere was electric!

Moo Salah had now fully recovered from his calf strain, and we had a full squad to choose from. We decided to stick with the side that had done so well in the last two league games. The only change was in goal, where Albert Ross came in for Jim Pan Zee, who was on the bench. We stuck to our trusty 5-3-2 formation.

Jack won the toss and chose to kick off. The referee (Mr James Mole) blew his whistle. It was 'Game On'!

The first meaningful attack came from Storkport, as their lone centre forward ran on to a long ball over the top and just got a shot in before he was closed down by Camelino. The shot lacked power though, and was comfortably saved by Albert Ross, a nice early touch for the rookie keeper. A busy and hectic 20 minutes had seen plenty of energy and commitment but little goalmouth action. Then, from nowhere, we took the lead. Marcus Ratface, a willing runner as always, had closed down one of Storkport's central defenders who had dwelt on the ball a bit too long. He nicked the ball off his hoof (the defender was a pony) and smashed the ball low into the bottom left corner from a tight angle. The keeper got a glove onto the ball but couldn't stop it going beyond him. 1 – 0 to Foalchester.

After the goal, the game opened up a bit more and there were a couple of decent chances at either end. Albert Ross was forced into a good low save, just getting a wing-tip to the ball and turning it around the post. At the other end, Rhinaldo had attempted a cheeky lob from 30 yards out having seen the keeper off his line. The ball had cleared the keeper but unfortunately the ball had just too much pace and dropped safely onto the roof of the net.

The game remained 1 – 0 with a few minutes plus additional time to play of the first half. We still led by the single goal, and it had been a relatively comfortable and controlled performance so far. We had kept the ball well and, without looking hugely threatening, there only looked like one team that were going to win this match. Us.

That was until the 2nd minute of additional time when from nowhere, Storkport got themselves back into the game through a highly controversial penalty given by referee Mole. Another long ball had been pumped over the top and the centre forward had just got a yard on Jack Longneck. The danger was quickly averted though, as Jack stretched out one of his famous long legs and took the ball cleanly and off for a corner kick. The referee blew his whistle and one of the Storkport players grabbed the ball ready to take the resulting corner. Then he, and several of the other players, saw that Mr Mole was pointing at the spot. He'd given a penalty! Not one player, including the Storkport players, had for one second thought that it was a penalty. Not even the Storkport *fans* had appealed for a penalty. Despite the protestations from our players, the ref was not about to change his mind. He'd also made another decision. He walked over to Jack and pulled out a card from his back pocket. It was red! Jack had been sent off, apparently for a professional foul. I was up on my hind legs on the touch line, snorting loudly through my nostrils. I couldn't believe it!

Pony Adams, who had earlier made the error for the Foalchester goal, bravely stepped up to take the spot kick. Albert Ross dived across to his right but the ball had been hit hard, straight down the middle. 1 – 1. A minute later, the whistle blew for half time. The referee was booed off by our fans but that wasn't going to change anything. From what had looked like being a fairly comfortable victory and smooth passage to the 1st round proper; we were now level and down to 10 men. The next 45 minutes would be crucial.

At half time we sat the players down for a breather and re-fuel before we talked about plans for the second half. I took Jack out for a quick chat about the best way forward. No doubt he was still angry and frustrated about his unfair dismissal, but he managed to stay calm on the outside.

The model professional. Between us, we agreed that we would have to sacrifice one of the forwards and bring on someone to drop into the centre of defence. We both agreed that the most natural replacement would be Moo Salah. Marcus had been causing most of the problems up front and

Moo Salah

Weight: 500 KG
Speed: 20 MPH
Height: 1.8 M

Favourite TV programme:
Moosround
Favourite celebrity:
Simon Cowell

Favourite food: Moosli
Favourite singer: Moodonna

Favourite songs:
The Green Green Grass of home,
This is How We Moo It

Favourite Joke:
What has 4 legs and says
"oom, oom"?
A cow walking backwards

had pace to burn so we decided to keep him on and to replace Kenny Dogleash. It was no reflection of Kenny's performance, but he understood the decision.

I then got the boys' attention and told them how we were going to line up for the second half and that we just needed to keep playing the way we'd been playing, and we could still win the game. The key was keeping tight at the back and playing more on the break. There was much talk of doing it for Jack, and Jack in turn told them how much faith he had in them. Now they had to go out and do the business!

Storkport had been buoyed by the sending off and knew that this was their big chance. They came out pumped up and full of energy. On 55 minutes they won a free kick just outside the box after a trip by Rhinaldo. Albert Ross set up a 3-man wall as the Storkport players lined up the free kick. One player feigned to shoot and jumped over the ball, the second curled a wicked right foot shot over the wall and towards the top, left corner. Despite his best efforts, Albert Ross couldn't get his long, left wing to the ball and it flew past him. It looked in; the crowd thought it was in; the players thought it was in; everyone in the ground thought it was in, but then it crashed on the inside of the angle where the upright and the cross bar met. It hit it with real force and bounced down just inches from the line. Harry Crane was quickest to the ball and managed to head it behind for a corner. A lucky escape, or so we thought. We'd heard the referee's whistle and had assumed that it was for the corner but then we saw that he was pointing to the centre circle and running back up the pitch. Unbelievably, he'd awarded the goal.

Some of our players rushed over to the assistant referee, Mr Bat. He soon held up his flag and waved it to get the attention of the referee. We were sure that he was going to inform him that the ball had definitely not crossed the line. But no! He was flagging because he believed that Lionelli had been too vociferous in his protestations (he'd argued too strongly!). The referee pulled out the yellow card and showed it to Lionelli who shook his head in disbelief. Somehow, we were 2 – 1 down, a player down, and staring an F.A Cup exit firmly in the face.

Partly due to the massive sense of injustice, and partly due to their never-say-die spirit, the team began to apply pressure on the Storkport goal. We were really fired up and playing some slick, neat football. It started to look like *we* were the team with the extra player. The Storkport manager responded to the increased pressure by bringing on another defender and withdrawing one of the attackers in an attempt to hold onto their lead. They managed up until the 78th minute when the pressure finally told. Chi Tah burst through from midfield and played a lovely reverse pass right into the path of the onrushing Marcus Ratface. Ratface took just one touch before rocketing the ball past the helpless keeper. 2 – 2 and very much back in the game. But no... the flag was up! Mr Bat again. Offside! Surely not...but it had been given.

As the clock ticked down to 85 minutes we made our final 2 substitutions, Zebrado coming on for Lionelli, and Ian Brush replacing Marcus Ratface who had just about run himself into the ground. There was still time.

Rhinaldo saw a left foot volley strike the post, and the Storkport keeper pulled off a miraculous save from a Camelino header. The 90 minutes was up. The board went up. There were to be 5 additional minutes to be played. Our supporters, who had not stopped singing and chanting all afternoon, raised their volume another couple of notches, urging on their team. All the Storkport players had got behind the ball and were desperately defending their goal. A high ball came into the area which Camelino, now playing as a makeshift centre forward, managed to get his head to. A Storkport defender flung himself across the goal line and blocked the ball with a raised arm just as it was heading in, and they managed to hack it clear. It had to be a penalty. Everyone looked round at the ref. We all waited for the whistle. After a moment's hesitation, the ref raised the whistle to his mouth and blew. A final chance to save ourselves. But to our dismay, the referee started walking towards the centre circle and collected the ball. At first, no one understood what was happening. Then it hit us; hit us like a speeding train. The ref had blown for the end of the game. It was over. The Cup run was over!

The referee and assistant referees were roundly booed off the pitch by the home fans. Then some of our players started to drift towards them including the rhino twins Rhinaldo and Rhinodinio who began to charge towards them. As quickly as I could, I ran onto the pitch, followed by Sid Silverback, and managed to block the charging rhinos, who both swerved around us and veered away from the officials. We understood their anger, but we had to get them calmed down as whatever action they took (flattening the officials into the ground seemed the most likely action!) it wouldn't alter the score or put us back into the cup competition. It was hard, very hard, but we had to take it on the chin and rise above it. Chi Tah was also shouting at the officials, as was Flamingo, but between myself, Sid, and Jack, who'd also run onto the pitch, we managed to usher them away and towards the tunnel. We needed to keep our heads.

Unfortunately, one member of the Foalchester staff let the side down. Me!! Having worked so hard to calm down all of my players, I'd then decided to rush over to the officials, bent my head down to go face-to-face with Mr Mole, and hit him with a barrage of rather poorly chosen epithets (in simpler terms, I swore at him!). He immediately reached into his back pocket and brandished the red card. I'd been sent off for foul and abusive language. I still wasn't going to leave it, but fortunately for me, Sid had got hold of me and pulled me away. I dragged myself away and headed for the tunnel. As I did so though, I heard shouting behind me. I turned and saw that Sid, having pulled *me* away, was now having a go at the officials himself. I rushed back to pull Sid off, returning the favour. As I manoeuvred him away, Mr Mole once more reached into his back pocket, pulled out the red card (again!) and pointed towards the back of the retreating Sid. A cup exit, 3 sendings off and probably a two-match ban for our captain, Jack Longneck. If a football season can be described, and I think it can, as a rollercoaster ride of emotions, then this was definitely the biggest and steepest drop!

Gazzer Grassnake & Jonjo Shellby
PODCAST

GG: Good evening and welcome to tonight's show.

JS: Yes, good evening.

GG: Before we discuss Saturday's defeat and cup exit to Storkport County, we want to inform you that we have some really big news to share with you later on in the show.

JS: Big, GG? It's huge. Massive. Gargantuan!

GG: Have you swallowed a thesaurus JS?

JS: A what? That's some kind of dinosaur, isn't it?

GG: I'll assume that's a joke JS. Anyway, as I say we've got some really big news later in the show.

JS: (Whispers) Ginormous.

GG: So, we must begin with Saturday's defeat. Big Jack sent off, Sid Silverback sent off, and the man himself, Horsé Marinio also sent off. What did you make of it JS?

JS: Well, firstly, I've got to say that the penalty and sending off of Jack was an utter disgrace. Mr Mole must have been the only person in the whole stadium who didn't see that Jack had clearly won the ball. Now, I realise that referees have tough decisions to make, and that it's a tough and pressurised job, but that decision was appalling.

GG: Yes, although I don't like to criticise officials, it has to be said that he had a shocking game. The only thing I would say is that he wasn't helped by the assistant referees either, especially Mr Bat. Why he couldn't see that the ball never crossed the line for the second goal I'll never know, he was directly in line with it. And the offside...

JS: Blind as a bat!

GG: A bit strong JS, but certainly another shocking mistake. And then of course we had the handball incident. Or not handball as the ref decided.

JS: Apart from catching the ball and juggling with it, it could hardly have been more obvious.

GG: Nicely put JS! With all of these incidents happening in one match, it was hardly surprising that our boys felt hard done by, but I didn't like to see some of our players confronting the officials.

JS: Emotions were high GG. I know how I was feeling as a spectator; must have been tough for the players to take.

GG: Agreed, but as a player you have to show a bit more professionalism JS. Certainly, Horsé and Sid Silverback should have shown more composure. Speak to the officials, yes, but not in that way. It looked bad JS.

JS: Yes. I agree on that one. I should just say that Horsé and Sid have both made public apologies for their behaviour. Hopefully, there'll be no further action necessary, and the club can move on.

GG: Now, moving on, we come to the news we spoke about at the start of the show.

JS: (Whispers) Monumental news.

GG: Indeed. Just before we came on air, we had a phone call from Pep Anaconda. He'd had a phone call from the Football Association regarding Saturday's match. *He'd* assumed that they'd wanted to talk about the incidents after the game and discuss possible consequences. But no. And this is the big news!

JS: Massive!

GG: The F.A had found out that one of the Storkport players – the scorer of their controversial goal as it happens – had not been officially registered with the club. As a result, they had no option but to void their victory. Meaning... Meaning...

JS: (Shouting) WE'RE BACK IN THE CUP!

GG: It's true! We're back in and through to the 1st Round Proper. Certainly not the way we would have liked to progress, but considering the manner of the defeat, it somehow feels like justice.

JS: Ditto. Couldn't agree more. Back in the hat!

GG: We're gonna leave you now and let you take in the announcement. Please feel free to contact us via phone or email with your opinions and questions. Until next week, goodnight.

JS: Goodnight. And a good night it really is!

CHAPTER 10 –
A PROPER FIRST ROUND PROPER!

Back in the hat we were! We'd got the team in early for training on a Tuesday night, so that we could watch the draw for the first-round proper. Our ball was ball number 40. All the big boys were in there with us, from Manechester United to Slitherpool. Pep had brought in a T.V, which had been set up in the bar behind our changing room. There we all sat, fingers crossed, tails crossed, legs crossed, wings crossed; whatever we had, they were being crossed. There was a huge amount of excitement amongst the group. Former players, Sheep Shearer and Peter Bearded Dragon were picking out the balls. "Number 34 – Crow Alexander are at home to – number 21 – Sowsend United." The draw continued, until fifteen ties had been decided. Several of the Premier League sides were still left in the bag, along with us. The excitement was mounting. "Number 17 – Manechester City" – we all crossed everything again – "to play number Forty" (Shearer coughs and apologises)," number Forty-Seven, – Swandon Town". A collective sigh went around the bar; so close. "Number 40" (we were at home!) – "Foalchester United... at home to... (everyone held their breath) – "Number 13 – Scrumthorpe Town." There was a disappointed groan amongst the players. Scrumthorpe were a professional team, currently sitting in 20th position in League Two, but it wasn't the big draw we'd all been hoping for. I'd been hoping for a big draw too, but I could also see that this was a big opportunity, firstly to play against a League side, but also a home game, and what I saw as a very winnable tie.

This was still a big game for the club and ticket sales were rocketing. Scrumthorpe were given 100 tickets, and the remaining 700 tickets were sold out within 2 days. The town was buzzing. The club was also to receive some television money as they were showing all the goals from the cup in a highlights programme in the evening. This was the first time there had been T.V cameras inside the ground, and a special scaffold tower had been erected especially for them (Pep had some contacts in the building trade). We'd even roped in the local Lion Cubs group to form rows either side of the tunnel, ready to give their loudest roars when the players ran onto the pitch. The big day was fast approaching, and we felt ready, on and off the field.

I had a full squad to choose from, with big Jack having served his two-match suspension for his sending off in the previous cup round. We'd lost one and drawn one in the League and had really missed his presence on the pitch. Jim Pan Zee had been meeting regularly with his therapist and was also attending a Bananaholics Anonymous group every Friday. He'd been making good progress and seemed much more focused and positive. For now though, I stuck with Albert Ross in goal who had done such a good job for us in Jim's absence. We'd trained and prepared well and were raring to go.

THE NATIONAL GAZETTE

JACK THE GIANT KILLER!!

Horsés Boys Do It Again!

A capacity crowd at the Mongoose Lane Ground watched on in soggy conditions as Foalchester United progressed into the next round with a hard-fought, narrow victory against Scrumthorpe Town from Football League Two. On a heavy, rain-sodden pitch reminiscent of cup ties from the past, the two sides fought hoof-to-paw with fierce tackling and big hearts. For a side newly-formed this year, this victory was quite some achievement against a full-time professional outfit.

In a tight game with few chances, it took a magnificent bullet-header from captain and ex-professional player, Jack Longneck, in the 57th minute to seal the 1 – 0 victory. In truth, there was little between the teams, and it was not obvious which of the teams was from the higher league.

Foalchester Manager, Horsé Marinio said that he was 'Delighted to get through to the next round' and heaped praise upon his team, with a special mention to 'Big Jack'.

The draw for the next round will take place after the completion of tomorrow's first round ties. No doubt they'll once again be dreaming of mixing it with the Big Boys!

By Cyril Stoat

A mention in the National Gazette! We were really starting to make people take notice. Foalchester United were making their mark!

The following day, the draw was made. I personally didn't see the draw as I was out with a group of my horsey friends playing a round of golf at the Hambleton golf club. Pep, although he didn't play himself of course, what with no arms, had managed to get me a membership of what was quite a prestigious club and I understood had a lengthy waiting list. I didn't ask him how he'd managed to wangle this one, but I'm pretty sure it had something to do with some contacts he had!

I was on the 15th hole when there was a buzz in my pocket, a text message. I knew immediately what it would be. Pep with an update. We'd been drawn away this time, away to Chimpwich Town of the Championship. Twenty or so years ago, they had been in the top league but had declined since and had spent several seasons in League 1. They had been through something of a resurgence in recent years and had been promoted last year. They were currently sitting just outside the playoffs in the Championship, having only lost four games so far this season. They also had an impressive stadium, Porkland Road, with a capacity of almost 25,000. They were well supported, averaging gates of over 17,000. It wasn't the dream draw, but it was certainly a good draw and a chance for us to compete against a good Championship side and in front of a sizeable crowd. I was sure that our own fans would come in good numbers as it was only about an hour away from Foalchester.

As I completed the last three holes, the phone kept buzzing in my pocket. I looked at a couple of the messages which were from some of the players, clearly buzzing as much as my phone. I switched my phone off for now and focused on my game. Unfortunately, my game didn't get any better though, as I came last out of the four of us, with an impressive 38 shots over par. Like any good golfer, I blamed my clubs rather than my complete lack of ability.

We had three league games to play before the next round of the Cup. With Injuries during these matches, and in training sessions, as well as some individual illness within the group, we had a fast-dwindling squad. Bill Badgerton, the physio, was suddenly rushed off his feet, doing his best to get players back onto the pitch. Some were just short-term injuries or illnesses. Terry Trotter had pulled a hamstring in training; Kenny Dogleash was being treated for worms; Moo Salah was having further trouble with his calf, and Marcus Ratface was recovering from food poisoning. Harry Crane was out for several months with a dislocated wing. With the next round of the Cup on the horizon – the biggest game of the season so far – we were suddenly down to the bare bones.

I decided to have a chat with Pep to see if there was any chance of bringing in any new players. We knew that it would be very difficult to make new signings in the short-term transfer window, especially at this stage of the season, but we could have more luck looking at a couple of possible loans. We'd met at his house, so he went and fetched his laptop, and we began to search the database for players currently on loan. With Kenny Dogleash and Marcus Ratface currently sidelined, we knew that at least one of the players needed to be a striker. They were going to be extremely hard to replace, with Marcus currently our top scorer with 13 goals, and Kenny not far behind on 11.

We sat together at the dining table trawling through the lengthy list of names. We were able to set a filter so that we could search for strikers only to begin with, but there were still hundreds of names to sift through. We made a short list of possibilities, twelve in all, so we could then research them individually in more detail. To save time, I used the internet on my mobile to research the first 6 names, while Pep researched the others on his laptop.

After a further half an hour or so, we had both chosen two possible loanees. We shared the names and showed each other some of the details that we had found. There seemed little to choose between the four, but we had to make a decision. Pep suggested that we both secretly write down the players in a list, starting with the most preferred, down to the least preferred. I wrote my four on a piece of paper and Pep, typed his out on his laptop, pressing the keys with his tongue. I handed him my piece of paper and came to take a look at his screen. The order didn't match, unsurprisingly, but fortunately our first choice was the same player. It was a young, up-and-coming player, currently playing in the reserve league for Premiership club, Toucanam Hotspur. A rabbit. His name – Bunny Sears!

We then began our search for a defender. We went through the same routine but this time we didn't agree on our first choice. After some discussion, Pep agreed to my choice as it would be me working directly with him. Again, he was a young player currently playing reserve team football with a Premier League club, this time Slitherpool. He was also another rabbit with the rather impressive name, Biffy Biffendale-Chops (not sure if we were going to manage to have his full name sewn onto the back of his shirt!) He could play in a number of positions and it was this flexibility that had caught my eye. He'd also played a couple of games for the England youth team.

Neither player had been involved in the Footballing Animals Cup games and would be eligible to play against Chimpwich Town in the next round. We'd never even seen them play, so it was certainly a gamble, but sometimes in life you just have to trust your gut and go for it! That's exactly what we did. Would the gamble pay off?

Bunny Sears

Weight: 1.75 Kg
Speed: 35 MPH
Height: 20cm

Favourite programmes:
Hay Duggie and
Bugs Bunny.

Favourite food: Carrots and
Hot Cross Buns

Favourite drink: Carrot Juice

Favourite singers or groups:
Echo and the Bunnymen and
Bunny Tyler

Favourite Joke:
What's invisible and smells of
carrots?
Rabbit farts!!!

Biffy Biffendale-Chops

Weight: 4.5kg
Speed: 30 MPH
Height: 22cm
Strengths: Fast over a short distance (powerful legs).

Expertise in: Binking.
(Jumping and twisting in the air to show happiness).
Once auditioned for Britain's Got Talent!

Your name sounds posh, are you from a wealthy background?:
You'll have to ask my butler!

Hobbies:
Tried horse jumping, but they were far too high!!
(ha, ha!)

Favourite Joke: How do you know that eating carrots is good for your eyes?
Have you ever seen a rabbit wearing glasses?

CHAPTER 11 –
CHAMPIONSHIP,
YOU'RE HAVING A LAUGH!

We arrived early at Porkland Road, and for the first time, Jack Longneck had come on the adapted team coach. A sliding panel had been built into the roof above the first seats on the driver's side. It meant that Jack only had to crouch down to enter the coach and was then able to put his head through the gap and take a seat. As long as the weather was ok, he'd be fine, and today, although quite chilly, it was a bright, sunny day with no rain forecast. There had been a slight delay when the coach was forced to go under a bridge on the outskirts of Chimpwich, but Jack had managed to manoeuvre himself to be a safe distance away from the top of the bridge. Most of the journey had been on dual carriageways and motorways, so they'd avoided passing overhanging trees.

As we approached the stadium, we were surprised at the size of the ground. It seemed massive compared to Mongoose Lane. For most of the players, Jack aside, this was all very new and exciting. The buzz around the coach was palpable.

We were shown through to our changing room, which was also highly impressive, and very spacious. There was still almost an hour and a half before kick-off, so we decided to go for a wander down the tunnel and onto the pitch, looking highly professional in the suits that Pep had got us fitted for. They must have cost a small fortune, what with all the different shapes and sizes of the players. Just the material for Rhinaldo and Rhinodinio's suits must have cost a tidy sum. I may have mentioned this before, but they were

BIG LADS! As for Elephantona... Well, enough said. No doubt Pep had some contacts in the tailoring business, but even so, he'd clearly spent a lot of his own money on fitting us out. The car-crushing business was clearly highly lucrative.

The pitch was like a bowling green. Short, emerald-green grass, a flat, rolled surface with perfectly painted white lines. It was quite a contrast from Mongoose Lane with its uneven, undulating surface and bare patches in the penalty areas and the centre circle. This would be great for playing football on, but playing on our own pitch may have given us an advantage, especially against a quality footballing side from the Championship. On top of that was the number of players we had missing. For the first time since starting on this journey with the team, I was feeling very anxious; worried that even with full commitment and endeavour, we may be outclassed. I had to put these thoughts to the back of my mind. Quickly.

It seemed to take an age, but finally it was quarter to three. Just time for a few more words of encouragement and instructions, and then we were out. We walked slowly down the tunnel, alongside the Chimpwich players, already hearing the roar of the crowd. As I led them out onto the pitch, I looked around and saw that the stadium was packed to the rafters. At the far end, to the right of the tunnel, our own supporters were making their own voices heard. We'd sold over a thousand tickets for the game, more than our own capacity. A lump rose in my throat and butterflies (not real ones, obviously!) started fluttering inside my belly. This was big. This was *really* big!

I'd decided to tinker with the formation, opting for 4-5-1. I just felt that we needed an extra player in midfield so that we could play a high-pressing game and try to stifle their more creative players. Albert Ross kept his place in goal, Camelino came in at Right Back, Flamingo at Left Back, Jack Longneck and Elephantona in Central Defence. Then in midfield, Zebrado, Left Wing, Chi Tah, Right Wing, and Rhinaldo, Rhinodinio and Lionelli in Central Midfield. Up front, playing the lone Striker role was Ian Brush. This only left Jim Pan Zee and new loan signings, Bunny Sears, and Biffy Biffendale-Chops on the bench. If I'd had fingers, they would have been firmly crossed, hoping for an injury-free game.

Jack won the toss. We were to kick off. The ref took one last look at both sets of players – then blew his whistle. We were away!

5 minutes in and we were a goal down! An uncharacteristic piece of loose marking had allowed Chimpwich's top goalscorer, Jason Gazelle to rise unchallenged at the far post and nod them in front.

Chimpwich Fans: "1 – 0 to the Chimpwich, 1 – 0 to the Chimpwich, 1 – 0 to the Chiiiimpwich!"

Still only 8 minutes on the clock when diminutive midfielder, Arnold Moorhen hit a speculative shot from over 30 yards out. He hit it well but straight at Albert Ross. Somehow though, the ball went straight through the Foalchester keeper's hands and into the back of the net. A dreadful individual error.

Chimpwich Fans: "Easy, Easy, Easy, Easy, Easy, Easy, Easy, Easy, Easy, Easy, Easy, Easy, Easy!"

It could hardly have started any worse, and I have to admit that I was fearing the worst.

On 25 minutes, 2 became 3. We'd won the header from their corner and got it some way out of the box. Good defending. But the ball dropped to Jason Gazelle who volleyed the ball first-time back towards goal. The ball flew off his hoof like a torpedo and crashed into the top corner between cross bar and post. A wonder goal! A Worldy as some people would say. 3 – 0 down and still only 25 minutes played. This could get embarrassing. The Chimpwich fans were loving it, taunting our own supporters.

Chimpwich Fans: "Can we play you every week? Can we play you every week? Can we play you, can we play you, can we play you every week? Can we play you every week?"

The odd thing was that there hadn't really been much between the teams, it's just that errors and a wonder goal meant that we were somehow 3 – 0 down. From the sideline, we shouted out encouragement and told the boys to raise their heads and keep playing. For the next 20 minutes the game settled down and we had, at least, not conceded any more goals. The board went up and there were to be an additional four minutes of play. We won a corner. Lionelli swung it in, as usual aiming for the head of Big Jack. He managed to get a slight flick on the ball but could not guide it towards goal. It bounced off the chest of one of the Chimpwich players and Ian Brush was onto it in a flash, stabbing the ball into the back of the net from close range. A typical, predator's finish from the 'Fox in the Box'! We'd got one back. We had a lifeline – a slim one, but a lifeline, nonetheless.

At half-time I drilled it into them that we still had a chance of turning the game around. The next goal was massive. If they scored, then it could be game over, if we scored then who knows? We needed to be tight at the back, strong in midfield and look to create a few chances. Above all, we needed to believe.

I sent the boys back out for the second half, pumped up and ready to give it their all.

Just four minutes into the second half however, we were dealt another blow. Lionelli and Rhinaldo had both challenged for the same ball inside the centre circle and had bumped heads. Lionelli, as you would expect, had come out much worse and blood was pouring from a nasty-looking gash across the bridge of his nose. Bill Badgerton, the physio, rushed on with his magic bag, pulled out the magic sponge and tried to work his magic. Lionelli made no fuss as he was tended to, but it was soon clear that he would need to come off, probably receive some stitches, and be checked over for concussion. His game was over. He was applauded off by both sets of fans and he left the pitch, helped off by the Rhino twins.

I needed to make a decision. After a quick chat with Sid Silverback, we decided to bring on Bunny Sears, but not as a direct replacement. Bunny was to go up front and support Ian Brush, as we moved to a 4-4-2 formation.

The game restarted with a drop-ball which Rhinaldo contested for us. The ball was won, and we played it around nicely, maintaining good possession. Chi Tah then received the ball in space on the right wing. He put on the afterburners and sailed past the Chimpwich left back before whipping in a dangerous ball into the area. Bunny Sears had made a darting run across to the near post and managed to flick the ball towards goal. It took a slight deflection off a Chimpwich defender and wrong-footed the goalkeeper. It was a goal! Bunny's first touch had been to put the ball into the back of the net, albeit from a slight deflection. 3 – 2 and it now really was 'game on'. The home fans were noticeably quieter, edgier, the chants now mumbles, recriminations and mutterings. Suddenly, they were nervous.

On 56 minutes, we were level! It was Bunny again, this time put through by Rhinaldo, and keeping his cool to bink the ball over the onrushing keeper. 3 – 3. The Chimpwich players looked shellshocked and had totally lost their composure. They were now making simple errors, committing silly fouls, and arguing amongst themselves. They were still a threat though, and almost regained the lead via a header from a corner kick. Albert Ross had to make a fantastic wing-tip save to keep it level. Most of the pressure, however, was coming at the other end. Zebrado picked up the ball on the halfway line and dribbled past two Chimpwich midfielders as if they weren't there. As he approached the box, he feigned to shoot, but instead played a lovely reverse pass to Ian Brush. He took a first-time snap-shot which the keeper did well to parry. With extraordinary speed, Bunny Sears was first to the rebound and smashed the ball into the roof of the net. It was 4-3 and Bunny Sears had scored a hat-trick on his debut. Now, could we hold on? Well, no, we couldn't hold on – we scored again!! On ninety minutes I'd decided to substitute Ian Brush (who'd run himself absolutely into the ground), for Biffy Biffendale-Chops. I'd also made the change to take up a bit more of the additional 5 minutes that had been added. On 93 minutes, with all the Chimpwich players pushing on in search of a last-minute equaliser, a long ball had been pumped forward into our box and was thumped away by Elephantona. Biffendale-Chops had kept himself just inside his own half and was now able to run onto the ball, defenders trailing in his wake. They were never going to catch him. Could he keep his cool? He nudged it forwards with his nose, keeping close control of the ball. Just the keeper to beat. The keeper, big David Seagull, spread himself wide in an attempt to block the oncoming rabbit, but Biffendale-Chops saw the keeper's legs open and nutmegged him expertly. He ran round the side of Seagull, who desperately grabbed Biffendale-Chop's shirt. It was a clear foul and surely a penalty, but Biffendale-Chops managed to stay on his feet and get a toe to the ball, the referee allowing him to 'play on'. The ball rolled into the empty net. 5 – 3 with just seconds to go. What a comeback!

On the sideline we were going wild. Sid was thumping his chest, I was standing on my hind legs neighing as loudly as I could, Jim Pan Zee had rushed out of the dugout and run down the line, doing front flips as he went. It was mad, crazy, fantastic!

Our fans were also going wild, chanting towards the Chimpwich fans.

"3 – 0 and you messed it up, 3 – 0 and you messed it up, 3 – 0 and you messed it up."

"Championship? You're having a laugh! Championship? You're having a laugh!"

We, players, and staff, went over to them to applaud them for all their support! What a moment! They were still singing when we'd left the pitch, gone down the tunnel and were back in the changing room. It felt like we'd already won the cup! We hadn't, but we were now into the last 16. Just how far could we go?

Zebrado

Weight: 400 Kg
Speed: 65 MPH
Height: 145 cm
Nickname:
Stripes (very original!)

Job:
Owner of hair salon 'Zebs'
Favourite singer:
George Zebra
Favourite sportsman:
Usain Colt (runner)

Favourite joke:
Why did the chicken cross
the road?
Because he saw the zebra
crossing!

(Well it makes me smile!)

Gazzer Grassnake & Jonjo Shellby
PODCAST

GG: Good evening and welcome once again to the Gazzer and Jonjo Podcast.

JS: Good evening.

GG: Well, JS, only one place to start – yesterday's amazing cup victory against Chimpwich Town!

JS: Amazing is about right an' all GG. Unbelievable! One of the greatest comebacks in the history of the cup.

GG: Probably *'the'* greatest JS, especially against higher opposition, a good Chimpwich side.

JS: Certainly didn't look likely after 25 minutes did it GG.? 3 – 0 down already – two of them from our own errors. Unfortunately, a real shocker from Albert Ross.

GG: I felt for him JS, I really did. I bet he just wanted the ground to swallow him up. He's done a fantastic job since he came in for Jim.

JS: Have to say, he showed a great attitude after the error. He held his wings up for the blunder but then re-focused well. Played a blinder after that.

GG: He did, JS, great attitude for a young lad. Could have let his head and beak drop, but he shook it off, and as you say, made some top saves after that.

JS: So, the comeback! Typical predator's goal from Brushy, the Fox in the Box!

GG: Just gave us a glimmer before half-time, didn't it?

JS: It did GG. But we still couldn't imagine what was to come in that second half. Crazy!

GG: Gave Horsé something to cling onto and he no doubt said that to the players. Another goal back and the game was back on.

JS: He certainly must have really geed them up during the break.

GG: Gee-geed them up!

JS: What?

GG: Gee geed them up!

JS: What are you talking about?

GG: Gee gee… it's a term for a horse… get it? Horsés a horse.

JS: Yes. I know…but I still don't know what you're talking about. Anyway, they came out flying in that second half, not literally of course cos that's against the rules, but they came out with renewed belief. And then it was 'Bunny Time'!

GG: You can say that again…

JS: Bunny time!

GG: What a debut. I've never seen anything like it. When we lost Lionelli, I have to admit that my enthusiasm and belief took a big knock. But… Bunny Sears had other ideas. Such clinical finishing.

JS: Incredible! I reckon Horsé may just have found himself a bit of a player, and even Biffy Biffendale-Chops managed to bag himself a goal on *his* debut.

GG: Could be huge signings JS. Anyway, I'm delighted to say that the hero of the moment, Bunny Sears has joined us in the studio. So, Bunny, firstly congratulations.

BS: Thank you.

JS: Congratulations from me too. What a debut! Did you ever even dream that you might score a hat-trick and play a massive part in putting Foalchester back in the hat for the next round?

BS: Yeah, no, to be honest Jonjo, not in my wildest dreams! I was just hopin' to get a few minutes on the pitch to be honest.

JS: And then, Lionelli takes a nasty knock and suddenly you're thrown on and given your chance to impress. I think we can safely say that that's exactly what you did!

BS: Yeah, no, for sure, to be honest it couldn't really have gone any better.

GG: For sure. You were such a livewire up there with Brushy. The defenders just couldn't handle you. Great pace and movement!

BS: Yes, no, yeah, it's how I play. High energy, lots of movement.

JS: Talking of energy, what the heck did you have for breakfast that morning?

BS: Hay.

JS: I said, what did you have for breakfast that morning?

BS: Hay.

JS: I said…

GG: Erm, JS, I think Bunny is saying that he had hay for breakfast.

JS: Oh… of course… sorry. What a twit I am!

GG: Well, I can't see anybody arguing with that!

JS: Cheers GG. So, Bunny, did you celebrate last night?

BS: Just a small glass of carrot juice.

JS: Special meal?

BS: Hey?

JS: Just hay again?

BS: What? No, sorry, I didn't hear what you said.

JS: Did you have a special meal last night?

BS: Oh, no, yeah, I did treat myself to a couple o' dandelions and a small tub of strawberry tops. Scrum!

GG: Sounds good, but not really my cup of tea.

BS: I didn't have any tea.

GG: Ok… Anyway, looking forwards, anybody you'd particularly like to get in Saturday's draw?

BS: Yeah, no, not really, one of the Premiership clubs would be good, but I'm not that bothered to be honest.

JS: Well, anyway, Bunny, thanks for coming in today and good luck in the league at the weekend. Maybe you'll get a starting place.

BS: Yeah, no, maybe, but that'll be up to the gaffer. I'll just do what I can whether I start or not.

JS: Thanks Bunny. That's the end of tonight's podcast, join us again next week.

GG: Goodnight, and up the U's!

CHAPTER 12 –
FOALCHESTER WILL PLAY…

The balls were emptied into the bag, and the bag was given a good shake up by feline singing sensation, Ollie Purrs, chosen alongside female pop star, Hyena Gomez, to make the draw for the last 16. Foalchester were ball number 8. They were the only non-league side left in the competition, with one team from League 2, one team from League 1, two teams from the Championship and the remaining eleven teams from the Premier League. The chances of getting one of the 'Big Boys' this round was much greater, and we were all hugely excited as the entire team and staff watched on from Pep's living room. All eyes were glued on the 56-inch plasma screen as Ollie shook the bag one final time, before dropping the balls into a clear, spinning cylinder. He gave the balls a few more seconds to mix up even more before finally being told to reach in and take out the first ball. As he held up the ball in his little paws, the commentator called out the number and corresponding team.

"Ball number 7, Manechester United, at home to…"

Hyena Gomez reached in to select the away team, rummaging deep into the pile of rotating balls. There was a buzz of expectation in Pep's living room as she pulled out her paw. She held it up.

"Ball number 6, Manechester City."

There was a loud mixture of oohs and aahs in the T.V studio as the draw threw up a Manechester derby in the Cup. In Pep's living room there was an outlet of groans and sighs as their anticipation and excitement seeped out, deflated. They were currently the biggest two teams in the

Premier League. Still, there were still some big names to go. It was Ollie's turn again. He straightened his whiskers, before once again delving into the remaining balls. He held up the next ball.

"Ball number 14, Stoat City, at home to…"

Hyena Gomez was next, her long claws sparkling with bright pink claw varnish, ready to dive back into the cylinder. She gave a big grin and a slightly peculiar laugh as she pulled out the next ball.

"Ball number 12, Slitherpool."

The draw continued in similar fashion, as we all sat nervously around Pep's living room. I remember having a quick look at the players and seeing Jim Pan Zee hiding behind his hands, Albert Ross flapping his wings nervously, Zebrado, tap-tap-tapping his hoof on the wooden floor, and even the usually super-cool Jack Longneck seemed to have lost control of his tongue, as it lolled about with a mind of its own. Poor old Jonjo Shellby could hardly bear to poke his head out from his shell. We waited and we waited. There were only two teams left and we were all trying to work out who it was. Then we found out.

"Ball number 13, Sowsend United will be at home to…"

"Ball number 8…" We all shouted with him, "Foalchester United!"

There was a collective groan around the living room. Sowsend? And away!

Now, I don't want this to sound like we've got anything against Sowsend, it just wasn't the big draw that we'd been dreaming of. Sowsend were a decent team, currently lying just outside the playoffs in League 1. It was a tough draw, especially away, but it obviously didn't have the glamour of playing against one of the big sides in the Premier League. Still, it was what it was, that's the cup. We had to get ourselves prepared and see if we could pull off yet another upset. Despite all that we'd achieved in the cup so far, we would still be very much the underdogs once again. Hopefully, we still had some bite left!

The Sowsend game was to be played on a Friday evening and was being shown on terrestrial T.V. Interest was huge, not just from the Foalchester supporters or people from around the area, but also nationally. The newspapers had begun to write a few stories about our group of part-timers who were taking the F.A Cup by storm, and I'd personally been interviewed by four of the tabloids, as well as appearing live on BBC radio. Our media team, Jonjo Shellby and Gazzer Grassnake, were being inundated with phone calls, letters, e-mails and texts. Everybody, it seemed, wanting to know more about our little club. All this exposure was fantastic for the club, helping to raise our profile and also bringing in a considerable amount of money; money that Pep had assured us would all go back into the club. We were feeling as though we were riding on the crest of a wave.

As the fixture approached, the excitement amongst the local supporters, as well as players and staff, was reaching fever pitch. Last 16 of the cup – live on T.V – it was barely believable. You could even see it in the face of Jack Longneck, old, seasoned pro that he was. Even he had never played in a game shown live on T.V before. It was strange to think that this fantastic stalwart of the lower divisions, who had retired from professional football, was suddenly caught up in the greatest cup run he'd ever been involved in. For the likes of the younger players like Marcus Ratface, Bunny Sears, and Albert Ross, it was almost too much to take in. I just hoped that the boys didn't freeze at the thought of potentially millions of people watching them perform. I knew how much nerves could affect even the most experienced players and had to try to keep them grounded, taking it as just another football match. That was easier said than done!

When it came to the selection of the team to face Sowsend, I had some very difficult decisions to make. In contrast to the previous round, we now had almost a full squad to choose from. Only Harry Crane, still feeling the effects of his dislocated wing, was doubtful, although even *he* had now returned to training and was ready, if required, to take his place on the bench. The toughest decision to make was who to start with up front. Bunny Sears had been the hat-trick hero of the previous round, but Kenny Dogleash, Marcus Ratface and Ian Brush, had all done brilliantly throughout the season. We also had Biffy Biffendale-Chops to consider. He could play up front as well as in defence, and had followed up his F.A cup debut goal with two more goals in league games. After a great deal of deliberation and several changes of mind, I finally decided to play Marcus and Kenny up front, mainly because I felt that they were a more tried and tested partnership.

I also had to decide on who else was to be in the starting eleven, who was to start on the bench, and, sadly, who was not going to be in the matchday squad. We now had 20 players signed on and were only allowed a maximum of five substitutes. Four players would have to be left out. The first two were not too difficult. Harry Crane, because he'd only just got back into full training, and Moo Salah who'd still got a troublesome calf that had meant missing a couple of games. Therefore, he was a bit lacking in match practice. My next decision was to drop Biffy Biffendale-Chops mainly because he was a loanee, and partly because he'd only been with us for a short time. The next one was the toughest of all as every single player had given their all for the club. Eventually it came down to a choice between two players, Adam Allama and Jim Pan Zee. Adam was a highly creative player and would be great to bring on if we were searching for a bit of inspiration from midfield. But, on the other hand, could I risk dropping Jim Pan Zee and not having a reserve keeper? I'd already decided that it was only fair to continue playing Albert Ross in cup games as he'd done so well for us, but dropping Jim from the squad altogether...? This was the part of management that I hated, but it was my job, I had to make tough decisions. Adam was in. Jim Pan Zee was out.

I announced the team to the players after training on the Thursday evening, having already had private conversations with those players who were regrettably going to miss out. They were tough conversations, but to my relief and admiration, the players took the news with great dignity and understanding. I knew my team; I knew my formation; I knew our tactics. WE WERE READY!

On Friday, we met at our ground where we were going to take the team coach. We'd all arrived in good time; all apart from Jim Pan Zee. Although he wasn't in the match day squad, he, and the other players outside the matchday squad, were still meant to be coming with us. Even if they were not playing in this particular match, we wanted to make sure that they were still involved and very much a part of the team. We waited for about 15 minutes, but still no Jim. We tried to contact him on his mobile, but calls just went straight through to his answer phone. It was too late to try calling round his flat, so we had to go without him. I just hoped that he was okay.

As we arrived at Coots Hall Stadium, there was already a large number of fans milling around outside the ground. Most of them were our own fans, proudly showing off the blue and white of Foalchester. There were still two hours before kick-off. It was a decent sized ground, holding 7500 fans, but it was very dated and looked a bit run down from the outside. Once we'd been led through and taken to the changing rooms, we took a stroll out onto the pitch. The stands were largely made of old, corrugated iron panels, held up by rusting metal pillars. It had clearly seen better days. The pitch though, looked in superb condition with just a little give in the ground from the rain we'd had earlier in the week. Whatever happened today, neither team would be able to blame the surface.

Just as we were about to go through the tunnel and back to the changing rooms, my phone vibrated in my pocket. I waited out on the pitch to answer it. I was surprised to hear the voice of Pep's wife, Anna Anaconda. Pep had travelled with us as usual, but had gone off to meet with the Sowsend chairman.

"Hi Anna, you ok? Pep's not here at the moment..."

"No, I know, I tried him, but he didn't answer. Anyway, it's probably you who needs to know..."

I didn't like the concern in her voice. She went on.

"It's about Jim Pan Zee..."

"Yes."

"I'm afraid he's been seen buying a large quantity of bananas in a supermarket in Wolfham Downs. One of the staff phoned the club as they'd heard about his problems. The girl that served him didn't know who he was and obviously thought nothing of a chimp coming in and buying bananas. It was one of the security guards that recognised him, but by then it was too late. Not that they could really stop him buying them. It's not like it's against the law."

"Oh, dear, that's worrying. Thanks Anna. Has anyone seen him since?"

"Not that I know of."

"Wolfham Downs? That's miles away from Foalchester. What the heck's he doing down there? Ok Anna, I'll have a think about what I can do. Thanks for letting me know."

What could I do? We were now only forty minutes away from kick-off. I decided to go and track down Pep and tell him the news. He told me that he'd try ringing around a few people and see if they could track him down. He had some contacts in the police force in Wolfham Downs (of course he did!!) and he'd ask them to keep an eye out for him. We both thought it best to keep this to ourselves for now, as we didn't want to burden the players so close to the game. I left Pep and went back to the changing rooms to deliver my pre-match speech. I could see in their faces that I hardly needed to say anything, the lads were clearly fired up and ready to go.

Jack won the toss, and we were to kick off. The atmosphere inside the ground was electric. Unsurprisingly, the game was a sell out and both sets of fans were in great voice. I couldn't help thinking of all the people watching the game live on T.V in pubs, clubs and living rooms. Little Foalchester United – quite remarkable!

The game started at a high tempo and tackles were already flying in. It was clear that neither team was going to pull any punches. With just over ten minutes gone, the first real chance was created, and it was Sowsend who almost took the lead. A free kick had been swung into the box and their number 9, Steve Bullo, had got away from his marker and flicked a header towards goal. The ball looped over the outstretched arms of Albert Ross, but Elephantona was well positioned on the goal line and flicked it away with his trunk. A close call!

The next chance came to us, in the 18th minute. A swift counter-attack had found Kenny Dogleash through on goal. Unfortunately, and uncharacteristically, Kenny took a heavy touch and allowed the keeper to close down the angle and make a good save at Kenny's feet. It remained 0 – 0.

Clear-cut chances remained at a premium, with solid, well-organised defences and hardworking midfielders keeping the game tight. On 45 minutes, Rhinaldo tried an audacious lob from almost the half-way line. He struck it well and it sailed over the goalkeeper who had positioned himself on the edge of the box. He was stranded and could only watch as the ball cleared him and bounced on the edge of the 6-yard box. Somehow though, the ball bounced up high and smacked against the crossbar, bouncing back out and rolling towards the mightily relieved goalkeeper, who grabbed the ball and held it thankfully in his arms. So close. The whistle went for half time.

Elephantona

Weight: Touchy subject! (I haven't been on any scales lately, but approximately 4,500 Kg)
Speed: 22 MPH top speed (generally nearer 5 MPH though)
Height: 3.1 m

Favourite holiday resort: Tuskany
Strengths: hard to knock off the ball.
Favourite films: Dumbo and Elephantasia
Favourite actor: Elephant Goulding

Favourite joke: Why do elephants have big ears? Because Noddy won't pay the ransom!!
(You do need to be of a certain age to get that one!)

I had a quick chat with Jack Longneck and Sid Silverback before giving my half-time team talk. I told the boys that we'd more than matched the Sowsend team and that we needed to keep up the work rate. I added that we could push up a few yards as a team and press a little bit higher up the pitch, but not to go chasing a goal and leave ourselves open to a counter-attack. Chances would come. There were no injuries, so I didn't see a need to make any changes yet. I then had a private word with Chi Tah who hadn't really been able to get into the game. I told him to take a gamble going forward, as Sowsend didn't seem to have a great deal of pace down the left flank, Chi Tah's right side. The buzzer sounded and we were back out for the second half. A big second half was needed.

On 54 minutes, Chi Tah received the ball on the right, he took off down the wing, leaving Sowsend's desperate challenges behind him. He reached the by-line and cut inside. He looked up and saw Marcus Ratface completely unmarked in the six-yard box. He swung a right front paw towards the ball but was clipped from behind by one of the Sowsend defenders. It was right on the line. Inside or outside the box? The referee took a look over at the assistant... and... pointed at the spot. It was a penalty. Despite the Sowsend protests (they surrounded the assistant referee, leading to two players being booked), the penalty had been given. This was a huge moment, especially in such a tight game. Rhinaldo grabbed the ball.

He placed it next to the spot and then nudged it delicately with his horn into the exact place he wanted it. He shuffled backwards on all four legs and then stood up on his hind legs ready for his run-up. This was always his method and it had served him well so far with six out of six penalties scored so far this season. He trotted forward on his back two legs and struck the ball with extraordinary power towards the goal. The keeper remained stuck to his spot. Suddenly, there was a loud "thwack" as the ball cannoned off the post and flew off towards one of the corner flags. One of the Sowsend players took no chances and knocked the ball out of play for a throw-in. Rhinaldo stood, head in hooves, consoled by the players around him. Suddenly though, Chi Tah sprinted at full speed towards the goal and crashed into the goalkeeper.

We couldn't believe our eyes! It was a ridiculous act and one that was sure to see a red card. Chi Tah, with Jordan Pigford folded up in his grip, smashed through the back of the net, just as the crossbar swung down towards the goal line. Rhinaldo's penalty had been hit with such force that the post had snapped in two and had, after remaining precariously balanced for a few moments, caused the crossbar to tumble downwards. Only Chi Tah had been alert enough, not just to see it, but to react to it. Amazingly, he'd probably just saved Pigford from serious injury or worse.

Players and staff from both teams, match officials and stewards, all rushed onto the field to make sure that everyone was alright, and that the situation was now ok. Chi Tah had let go of Jordan Pigford and both were now on their feet, seemingly uninjured. Chi Tah received enormous praise for his actions; deservedly so. Once the situation was calm, the referee blew his whistle and asked the players to leave the field of play and go back to their changing rooms while a new goal was put in place. Ground staff were already on their way to dismantle and drag away the broken goal and had a goal ready to be brought in from an area behind the corner of the stadium. It had been used during the warm-up. What they'd have done otherwise I really don't know. Maybe take the other goal off and use jumpers for goalposts! Anyway, it gave us another chance to get together, get some liquid on board, and make any little tweaks that might be needed.

Around 15 minutes later, the teams were back on the field and ready to re-start the match. We started back where we'd left off, with a throw to us, but we decided to throw the ball back to their goalkeeper and start from there. A ripple of applause rang around the stadium. The game was back on. We seemed rejuvenated from the break in play and soon took control of the game. We kept the ball well and started to pressurise the Sowsend goal. Jordan Pigford was forced into a couple of excellent saves, one from a Marcus Ratface volley

Chi Tah

Weight: 51 Kg
Speed: Up to 105 MPH
Height: 75 cm

Nickname: Lightning, Whizzer
Dislikes: Cheaters
Strengths: Incredible Pace

Favourite singers:
Ollie Purrs, Kitteny Spears,
Hyena Gomez, Catty Perry

Historical hero:
Cheetah The Great
Favourite film:
The Fast and the Furriest!

Favourite Joke:
What side of a cheetah has the
most spots?
The outside!

and one from a piledriver from Rhinodinio. Sowsend were struggling to withstand the pressure and couldn't really get the ball away, but they did defend resolutely, throwing themselves into blocked challenges and making last-gasp tackles.

With ten minutes plus injury time to go, I made my first changes, bringing on Bunny Sears for Marcus Ratface and Adam Allama for Lionelli. They were straight swaps but offered us fresh legs and a little more creativity in midfield. Within five minutes of coming on, Adam Allama received the ball in the middle of the centre circle and played a first-time, slide-rule pass through to the speedy Sears. Sears took a touch forward and sped towards goal, defenders desperately, and hopelessly, trying to get back. The keeper came out to narrow the angle, but Sears stood up on his back legs and tricked the keeper into thinking he was going to shoot. The keeper dived down to his left as Sears swerved around the keeper's right and calmly rolled the ball into an empty net. In the away fans area, our fans were going crazy! At last, the pressure had told, and we found ourselves deservedly one goal up. The substitutions couldn't have worked better. Now we just needed to see out the final five minutes and injury time.

I told the players to keep up the intensity and work rate and not to sit back and hold on for the final whistle. We continued to dominate possession and a tiring Sowsend United were struggling to get a hold of the ball. The board went up. three more additional minutes to play. As Sowsend threw caution to the wind, sending both centre backs up front, Chi Tah ran on to another through ball from Adam Allama and ran through to neatly finish past the helpless Pigford. 2 – 0 and the game was over. We were through to the quarter finals. The dream was still alive and breathing!

Having congratulated the players and joined them as they went over to applaud our fantastic band of supporters,

I heard my phone buzz in my pocket. I waited until the players had left the pitch before checking it. I clicked on my voicemail message. It was Pep. There was news of Jim Pan Zee. He'd been found slumped on a bench at Wolfham Downs Station, reportedly surrounded by empty banana skins. The joy of the victory was suddenly tainted by the knowledge that Jim had had a relapse in his fight against Bananaholism. If I'm honest, I had feared that that may be the case when he hadn't shown up. I couldn't help thinking that my decision to drop him from the match squad may well have caused, or partly caused, the relapse. I stood by my decision, the way the match had panned out showed it to have been correct, at least from a footballing side. I still felt, and still feel to this day, that I should have recognised the effect that being dropped may have had on him and should have given him more support. I'd been fooled by the professional and calm way that he'd initially taken the news.

I phoned Pep back and was told that he'd managed to get Jim into a rehabilitation clinic. He was being carefully monitored but he was not in any serious physical danger. Pep had spoken to the staff at the clinic and had been told that the young lad was now fast asleep, having been given a mild sedative. He'd booked him in for a week to begin with to see how he reacted to treatment. It was currently the right place for him.

The joy of the victory; the ecstasy, had been completely overshadowed by this sobering news. I phoned Sid Silverback, currently with the players in the changing rooms, and told him that something had come up and I'd decided to go back with Pep. I didn't tell him why. Letting them enjoy their amazing victory. Pep and I headed straight off to the clinic.

CHAPTER 13 –
THE GOOD NEWS, THE BAD NEWS, AND THE QUARTER FINAL

THE RATTLER

HORSÉS HEROES!

Horsé Marinio's Foalchester United have continued with their amazing cup run with a comfortable 2 – 0 victory against League 1 Sowsend United and are now set for the quarter finals. And lightning-quick winger, Chi Tah, performs his own heroics in another extraordinary chapter in this ongoing sporting saga.

There followed the full match report and a separate section showing and describing the incident involving Chi Tah and Jordan Pigford. The photographer had brilliantly captured the moment when Chi Tah had launched at Pigford just before knocking him back into the goal. It proved to be a photograph that the photographer would go on to win many awards for, including Sports Photo of the Year. We were genuinely big news now and I remember feeling so proud when reading the articles. Little old Foalchester spread across the whole back page of several national newspapers.

Sadly though, one of the papers had other stories to tell. They still put us on the back page; full match report; detailed account of the Chi Tah incident; praise etc. But this paper, The Daily Lion, had also splattered us across the front page. It showed an image of Jim Pan Zee draped across a bench at

Wolfham Downs Station. Clearly, somebody from the public had recognised Jim and had taken a photo of him hoping to make a bit of money selling it to the papers. The Daily Lion, well known for its trashiness, had obviously jumped at the chance. 'Back on the Bananas', the headline read. Followed by the sub-heading 'Shame of Footballing Chimp', which then led to a shocking article about Jim's bananaholism, about the club's failure to deal with the issue, about Jim's conduct, and about him being a poor role model to children, many of whom now saw him as a hero. It had even dredged up details about Jim's father who, unbeknown to us, had also struggled with banana addiction. This is where Jim's issues stemmed from according to the paper, or as they put it 'A Chimp off the Old Block'. It was an article full of falsities, exaggerations, supposition, and complete and utter lies. It was the gutter press at their very worst and so typical of The Daily Lion, Lion by name and Lyin' by nature. I was fuming, as was Pep when he rang me up later that morning. Pep took it upon himself to ring the paper and lodge a complaint, whilst also asking for an apology to be printed the very next day. They refused and accused Pep of interfering with the Freedom of the Press. Pep even threatened to take legal action (and no doubt he had a number of contacts in the Law profession), but they simply told him to 'do his worst'.

The following day, the latest issue of The Daily Lion came out. On the front page was a new headline, once again followed by a large photograph. This time the photograph was of Rhinaldo and Rhinodinio, and the headline read 'Horsés Heroes or Villains?' Followed by the subheading, 'Rhino Twins Criminal Past'. Aggrieved by the criticism from myself and Pep, the paper had decided to wage war against Foalchester United and had immediately gone about digging up some dirt about some of our other players. The article recounted the armed robbery that the two lads had carried out, focusing on the devastating affect it had had on those who had been threatened. No doubt there was a sizeable amount of truth in what they said, and the details of the robbery were correct, but it had been worded so as to make out that the two rhinos were habitual, hardened criminals, who had shown little or no remorse for their actions. We all knew that that was far from the truth. The gloves were off, and the paper was fighting dirty!

Whilst all this was going on, the quarter final draw was fast approaching. Our league form had dropped off a little, with a defeat and two draws in our last three games, partly I believe due to the negative publicity from The Daily Lion. Clearly, Rhinaldo and Rhinodinio had been affected, with Rhinaldo almost as quiet as his always shy and introverted brother. Neither of them managed to keep up their normally high standards and several times I had to either replace one of them, or start one of them on the bench. For a couple of huge, powerful rhinoceroses, they were inwardly very sensitive and despite the efforts of the other players and the staff, me included, it was hard to get them fully focused and motivated. Their mood affected some of the other players too, some feeling sad for them, others angry at the newspaper. All this was coupled with concerns for Jim Pan Zee, who had remained in the clinic receiving treatment. Lionelli allowed his anger to spill over in one of the league games and he took it out on an opposition defender, lunging in with an overly aggressive and dangerous tackle that earnt him a red card. He would now miss the cup quarter final. It was a tough, challenging time for the club and for me as manager. The toughest so far.

The draw was made in the BBC studio on a Sunday evening by two of the England women's team players, Jess Carthorse and Ella-Phant Toone. Just eight balls left, and we were one of them! The other seven teams were all playing in the Premier league so whichever number we were drawn against it was going to be massive for us. We had all got together round Pep's again to watch the draw live.

"Number 3." That was us. First ball out. A home draw!

"Will play..."

The balls spun round inside the cylinder.

"Will play... Wimbledogs."

There was a mixture of cheers and groans as the name was read out. They were a Premier League club, currently lying in 12th place in the league, but they were well-known for their aggressive, take-no-prisoners attitude. Their captain, Vinnie Bones (a Staffordshire Bull Terrier), was a no-nonsense midfielder with a reputation for intimidating opposition players. He'd been sent off 14 times in his professional career and picked up numerous bookings. Much of Wimbledog's success had come from their hard tackling and physicality, but they could also play some decent football. One thing was for sure, they were going to provide really stiff opposition and we were going to have to be at our best, and not let ourselves get involved in any unsavoury incidents. I have to honestly say here, that I was slightly relieved that Lionelli was going to miss this game through suspension. He was a great, hardworking, hard-tackling player, but he was apt to react to opposition goading or bad tackles and the Wimbledog's players would undoubtedly have targeted him. That said, he'd still be a big miss.

The game was scheduled to kick off at 5.30 p.m. on a Sunday and was once again being screened live on the BBC. Pep had arranged for extra, temporary seating to be added to the ground, which brought the capacity up to 1500, but we could have sold more than 10 times that amount easily. Wimbledogs had been allocated 300 tickets which had been sold in seconds on their website. Another full house was guaranteed. Pep had also organised a big-screen showing of the game live in Foalchester Public Gardens, free of charge for those unable to secure tickets.

In the league, we'd won our previous two games, 1 – 0 and 2-1 respectively and were clearly returning to good form. On the injury/sickness front, Camelino had mumps (and humps!), Zebrado was suffering from a fetlock strain and Moo Salah was once again having trouble with his calf. Obviously, we also had Lionelli suspended. On a more positive note, Jim Pan Zee had now completed his time at the clinic and was once again available. I must say that he was looking much more himself and it seemed that the treatment he'd received at the clinic had worked wonders, (I hoped it would last).

We set up as follows, reverting once more to our favourite 3-5-2 formation.

1. Albert Ross – Goalkeeper
2. Biffy Biffendale-Chops– Central Defender (Right)
3. Jack Longneck – Central Defender (Centre)
4. Terry Trotter – Central Defender (Left)
5. Rhinaldo – Central Midfield
6. Rhinodinio – Central Midfield
7. Harry Crane – Right Wingback
8. Chi Tah – Central Midfield
9. Kenny Dogleash – Striker
10. Marcus Ratface – Striker
11. Flamingo – Left Wingback

Subs: Adam Allama, Eric Elephantona, Bunny Sears, Jim Pan Zee, Ian Brush

The fans from both sides were in full voice and a fantastic atmosphere was created. Mongoose Lane was bouncing (quite literally where a group of Kangaroo school children were standing!) The referee checked his watch, checked with his officials, and blew the whistle. We were away. Within two minutes, Bones thundered into his first tackle, winning the ball off Flamingo but following through to take the player out too. No foul, according to the referee, Mark Cattenburg. John Fash-Emu was next to fly into a tackle (not literally of course!),

Terry Trotter

Weight: Less than Elephantona!
(Approximately 250Kg)

Speed: 8MPH (at a push!)
Height: 82 cm

Favourite films:
The Harry Trotter films.

Hobbies:
Eating. Digging truffles.

Favourite sport:
Except football – Pig Pong

Favourite books:
Animal farm and Babe

Favourite joke:
What do pigs use for dry skin?
Oinkment!

Harry Crane on the receiving end this time. A free kick was given, and the ref had a quick but stern word with Fash-Emu. It was some 30 yards from goal but definitely within the range of either Rhinaldo or Rhinodinio. Rhinodinio ran towards the ball but jumped over it at the last minute, moving out of the way to his right, Rhinaldo ran in and blasted a pile-driver over the wall and towards the top left corner. It looked for all the world that it was in, but somehow the Wimbledog's keeper, Dave Pheasant, managed to get a couple of tail feathers to the ball and diverted it just enough to crash against the crossbar. A fantastic save. Still 0 – 0 with twelve minutes played.

Wimbledogs were next to create a chance. A long ball from Bill Bison had been won in the air by Fash-Emu, who had managed to nod it into the path of Dennis Sties. Sties hit a first-time shot which Albert Ross did well to turn around the post. From the resulting corner, Phil Jaguarelka managed to leap up ahead of Jack Longneck and angled a header towards goal. Fortunately, the close attention of Jack had meant that Jaguarelka hadn't got much power into the header and Albert Ross had made a comfortable save.

With twenty five minutes on the clock, a pin-point through ball from Rhinodinio set Kenny Dogleash away, with only Bulldog Bremner anywhere near him. There was no way that Bremner was going to catch the fleet-footed Dogleash, so he opted for grabbing his tail, clearly pulling him back. Being one-on-one with the keeper it had to be a free kick, but even more importantly, a sending off. The whistle blew and we just waited for the ref to show the inevitable red card. The referee reached for his pocket and... produced a yellow card! Even the Wimbledogs players, Bremner included, looked amazed at the decision. It was the most obvious professional foul that I'd ever seen; it was one of the worst decisions I'd ever seen, and from such a well-respected referee. We just had to rise above it, get back, and focus on the game.

On 35 minutes, Wimbledogs had forced a corner; they'd already looked dangerous from a corner early in the match. Ray Crab took the corner and swung his left pincer hard to curl the ball to the back post. Don Key, up from the back, managed to get his head to it and powered his header towards the top right corner of the goal. Somehow, Albert Ross managed to get across and throw a desperate wing at the ball, which struck the woodwork where bar and upright met. The ball rebounded towards the penalty spot where Ronnie Rottweiller met it with a thumping volley. A well-positioned Terry Trotter managed to block the ball on the line with his belly but could only watch as the ball dropped down to the waiting Harry Hyena, who nudged the ball into the back of the net. It was a typical scavenger's finish from Harry Hyena, known for feeding on scraps in the box. It was his 14th goal of the season and not one of them had come from outside the area. Despite the heroics of Ross and Trotter, we were 1 – 0 down, slightly against the run of play.

The second yellow card of the game came in the 39th minute, with Denis Sties unceremoniously upending Chi Tah as he skipped easily past him. From the ensuing free kick, Rhinodinio got us back into the game with a superb, swerving shot that curled around the wall and flew past the outstretched wing of Pheasant in goal. 1 – 1 and all to play for.

There was a scrappy period of play after the equaliser, with a number of petty fouls and some play-acting from several Wimbledogs players. It was obvious that they just wanted to get to half time on level terms. They almost came unstuck though, as a cheap free kick was awarded to us wide of the 18-yard line. Crane took it and curled a dangerous ball into the box, with whip and pace. It just needed a good touch towards goal. Jack Longneck easily won the header and crashed it into the back of the net. 2 – 1, or so we thought. But the assistant referee was frantically waving his flag at the referee, who blew his whistle and ran over to confer with his colleague. After a long chat, the referee blew his whistle again and pointed for a free kick to Wimbledogs. There was no doubt that Jack had won his header cleanly, but we were told at half time that the assistant referee had seen an infringement by Kenny Dogleash as the ball had come into the box. Nobody else had seen it, and when we watched back the game on T.V later that evening we couldn't see anything other than the usual bit of pushing and shoving in the box. If anything, it looked like one of the Wimbledogs players had hold of Kenny's shirt. Anyway, it was done, and we went in on level terms, still very much in the game.

At half time I sat the players down in the changing room and made it clear to them that we had controlled most of the game and were unlucky to be coming in only level. I also reminded them just how important it was that we all kept our discipline and didn't let Wimbledogs bullish behaviour get to us. We needed to keep eleven players on the pitch. There were no injuries and there was no reason to make any changes at this stage. We just needed to keep going the way we had been, and the goals would come. We just needed to be patient. I also had a quick, quiet word with young Marcus Ratface who had borne the brunt of some very physical challenges. I told him to think of it as a compliment that they felt that that was the only way that they could stop him. Jack also chipped in with his own advice to the team, having faced many highly physical teams during his professional career. He really was an amazingly inspiring captain, not just because of his height and natural presence, but his general manner and strong leadership qualities.

The referee blew the whistle for the start of the second half, a big 45 minutes to come. Within a couple of minutes, it was clear that Wimbledogs had no intention of changing their manner of play, with Don Key upending Marcus Ratface after being nutmegged by the skilful rat. It was an immediate booking, but more worrying was the fact that Marcus was still on the ground. Bill Badgerton sprinted onto the pitch, medical kit strapped to his shoulders, ready to check on Marcus's injuries. After a couple of minutes, Marcus was back on his feet but had to go off the pitch before being allowed back into the game. Soon he was back on, although not yet moving comfortably. Bill told me that Marcus had been caught in the ankle, but it was only a bit of bruising, and he should be able to run it off. Unfortunately, though, Marcus wasn't given any time to recover or run it off, as Vinnie Bones crashed through him with another scything tackle. A simple decision for the referee, a yellow card, but Marcus had been caught once again on his ankle and was clearly in a lot of pain. I told Bunny Sears to start warming up as Bill Badgerton was once again called onto the pitch. This time, it was clear that Marcus was not going to be able to continue and he was sadly taken off the pitch on a tiny stretcher. Our fans gave him a huge ovation as he was stretchered off and taken down to the changing rooms; there were tears in his eyes. Bunny Sears took off his sweatshirt and took up his position alongside Kenny Dogleash.

Sears was immediately into the action as he ran onto a lovely through ball from Flamingo. His electric pace had left the defenders floundering behind, and he was right through on goal with just Dave Pheasant to beat. Pheasant did his best to narrow the angle, waving his wings up and down to try to put him off, but Sears kept steady and side-footed the ball past the flailing keeper. We'd deservedly got ourselves in front. 2 – 1 to Foalchester.

We continued to dominate the game with slick, accurate passing, frustrating the Wimbledogs players who could not even get close enough to put in a serious challenge. There was plenty of frantic effort, with Bob Catt and Ronnie Rottweiller above all putting in a real shift for 'The Dogs', but even they couldn't disturb our control of the game. Only some excellent goalkeeping from Dave Pheasant and some desperate last-gasp blocks were keeping Wimbledogs in the game. They were dropping deeper and deeper as a team and were struggling to get the ball out of their half. Even when they did, there were no strikers left up front and the ball would just

Flamingo

Weight: 3Kg
Speed: 15 MPH
(Running, not flying!)
Height: 1.5 M

Favourite colour: Pink
Job: Dance instructor
(mainly ballet)

Strength: Elegant, graceful
ball player.
Weakness: a bit one-legged
at times!

Favourite Singer:
Placido Flamingo

Favourite joke:
Why does a flamingo stand
on one leg?
Because if it didn't it would
fall over.

come back at them again. Surely the third, and almost certainly, winning goal, was only a matter of time away.

But the third goal alluded us, despite all our efforts. Sears hit the bar on 78 minutes and Rhinaldo blasted a shot, inches wide, from outside the area on 82 minutes. From a corner in the 90th minute, there was an almighty scramble as the ball dropped near the penalty spot. As we tried to scramble the ball over the line, the 'Dogs' defenders were throwing themselves at us to block. The ball was pinging around like a frenzied pinball machine, but the ball just refused to go in. Eventually, the ball dropped close enough to Dave Pheasant for him to dive gratefully onto it. He stood up and waved his players forward, time was running out, the board had shown 7 minutes of injury time. He punted the ball up well beyond the half-way line where Fash-Emu won the header. The ball landed in the path of Ray Crab, who ran sideways to the left, then sideways to the right, then sideways to the left again, before finally passing sideways to Dennis Sties. Sties cleverly shielded the ball from the onrushing Crane and bought himself a free kick close to the touch line, roughly 35 yards from goal. This was their last chance and they even sent Pheasant, the goalkeeper, up to make a nuisance of himself in the box. Sties set the ball down, ready to take the freekick himself. He bent in a wicked ball which Albert Ross decided to come for. The box was so packed though, that the path to the ball was crowded and he ended up running into the back of Big Jack. He still managed to get a wing to the ball, but he couldn't hold it. The ball hit Bill Bison on his rather ample backside and rolled into the six-yard box where the scavenger himself, Harry Hyena, was once again waiting to crash the ball into the net from close range. From almost nothing, they'd equalised. 2 – 2 and the whistle went almost immediately after the restart. Extra time loomed!

We quickly got the boys rehydrated before commencing the team talk. I'd been chatting to Sid about the best way forward for the extra time. We still had four substitutes if we wanted to change things around. We decided to change Kenny Dogleash for Ian Brush and Rhinodinio for Adam Allama. As usual, Kenny had worked his paws off up front, but had just started to tire towards the end. Rhinodinio had picked up a bit of a knock late in the second half and wasn't moving comfortably, so that was an easy decision to make. 30 minutes left. 30 tense, nervous minutes.

Wimbledogs kicked off but had soon squandered possession with Rhinaldo robbing Bones of the ball and leaving him in a heap on the floor. It had been a perfectly fair tackle, but Bones was clearly angry. He'd sprung back up and chased after the marauding Rhinaldo. He flew into the back of Rhinaldo with a dreadful four-footed tackle, but on this occasion, he'd bitten off more than he could chew, and he just simply bounced off the thick hide of the Rhino's rump and crashed down onto the hard surface. This time he'd injured himself and rolled around in pain, barking, and whimpering loudly. It was hard to tell if he was genuinely injured or not, as he may have been feigning injury so that the ref would forget about his shocking challenge. Injured or not, Mr Cattenburg was already standing over him. He reached into his pocket and pulled out... a yellow card! We couldn't believe it; even the Wimbledogs players looked stunned. Bones, himself, got quickly back to his feet and, with a big grin all over his face, rejoined the action. Somehow, he'd got away with a challenge that he could have been arrested for, let alone sent off!

Wimbledogs were playing very deep by now, with often all of their players behind the ball; they were just hoping to hang on for the penalty shoot-out. They'd also started using time-wasting tactics, with players suddenly collapsing to the floor in need of medical attention, some complaining of cramp. They were taking a long time over throw-ins and free kicks. Corners were being played short and they would try to hold the ball near the corner flag. Little niggly fouls were also being committed, anything just to stop the game flowing. They were doing a good job of stopping us getting any meaningful attacks together, limiting us to speculative shots from long range. The first half of extra time was already up and neither team had created anything like a decent chance.

The second half of extra time started in exactly the same fashion, with Wimbledogs defending in numbers and simply thumping the ball forward or off the pitch, then re-setting ready for our next attack. It was like an attack versus defence training drill. In the ninth minute of the second half of extra time, Adam Allama managed to dink a neat little ball into the paws of Ian Brush, just inside the box. He rose up on his two back legs, flicked the ball up and performed an incredible bicycle kick. In the dugout we were all up out of our seats ready to celebrate, but then we heard a loud thump as the ball clattered against the inside of the post and bounced back out, just eluding Bunny Sears's outstretched back legs and finally being booted out to safety by Dog's defender, Don Key. So close!

With two minutes to go, we won a corner kick and Jack and Biffy Biffendale-Chops had been waved forward. Only Trotter stayed back to keep an eye on the loan striker, Fash-Emu. Allama took the corner, but he didn't manage to clear the player stationed at the near post, who volleyed the ball up the pitch. Trotter, defending near the half-way line, stepped forward to attack the ball, but he misjudged its flight and the ball landed a couple of feet in front of him and bounced over his head. Fash-Emu was quickly onto the error and burst away towards goal. He was very quick, but also rather gangly and awkward-looking and he never seemed to have the ball fully under control. He then took a heavy touch and Albert Ross, our keeper, rushed out of his area and bravely dived onto the ball just inside the area. Fash-Emu, frustrated no doubt by his heavy touch, still went sliding in at Ross with a truly horrific challenge. There followed a frantic and highly charged melee on the pitch as players from both teams ran across to the incident. Fash-Emu was already walking off the pitch before Cattenburg had even shown him the red card. Ross was still on the ground, blood trickling down his thin, spindly legs. It looked bad, but once Bill had inspected it, he could at least assure us that there were, fortunately, no broken bones. Sadly though, there was also no way that he could continue. I looked over at Jim Pan Zee.

"You ready Jim?"

The referee blew the final whistle. Penalties! I called the players over into a huddle and asked for volunteers for the penalty shoot-out. We'd already got a list down in case the game went to penalties, but we just needed to be sure that everyone was still ready to take them. It was high pressure. A place in the semi-final of the F.A Cup was at stake. Every single hand, leg, or wing went up, even Jim's; I felt so proud of them. Our captain, Jack Longneck, and Wimbledogs captain, Vinny Bones were called over and the referee tossed the coin in the air. Jack called Heads; Heads it was, Jack chose for us to go first. Jack, himself, was to take the first penalty.

He placed the ball on the spot and took a couple of steps back, looking as cool as he always did. We watched on from the half-way line, all linked together, as this magnificent giraffe strode majestically forward. Pheasant was moving up and down the goal line in an attempt to put him off. Bang! Jack crashed the ball low into the goalkeeper's right-hand corner. 1 – 0. Never in doubt!

Jim made his way to the goal and set himself. First up for Wimbledogs was Harry Hyena, their usual penalty taker. He took a short run up and slotted the ball to the keeper's left, cleverly sending Jim the wrong way. 1 – 1.

Next for us was Rhinaldo. He put the ball on the spot and took a long run up. Pheasant, in goal, looked as though he wanted to be somewhere else. The huge, muscular rhino stampeded forward, and ... dinked the ball down the middle of the goal, with Pheasant diving to his right, diving just to get out of the blast that he was expecting. Astonishing coolness from the big man!

Next up for the Dogs was Denis Sties. He nudged the ball onto the spot with his snout and took a few steps back. Up on his back legs, he trotted, (or trottered) forward and slammed the ball towards Jim's left-hand, bottom corner. He'd struck it well, but Jim had guessed the right way and somehow managed to get a couple of fingers of his favourite 'banana'-style gloves onto the ball and did just enough to divert the ball onto the post. Sties covered his face with his front trotters. It was 2 – 1. First blood to us.

Brush was next, with a chance to put us 3 – 1 up. Pheasant was again moving along the goal line, waving his wings in an attempt to put off the taker, but Brush just ran up and nonchalantly side-footed the ball into the bottom left of the goal. Pheasant had hardly moved. 3 – 1 to Foalchester.

Don Key was next for the Dogs. He placed the ball on the spot, then stood with his back to the goal, with the ball right behind him. Jim didn't understand what was happening and wasn't really ready, as Key kicked backwards with his hind legs and thumped the ball into the back of the net like a guided missile. It was extraordinary! He literally kicked like a mule! 3 – 2.

Harry Crane was our fourth penalty taker. As he made the long walk from the centre circle to the penalty area, the Wimbledog's fans (the penalties were being taken at their end), raised the noise even more, with whistles, chants, and boos. He nudged the ball forward with his long, stick-like legs, then turned and took five paces back. He looked towards the goal, moving his head from one corner to the other, and again, and again. It was as though he was toying with Pheasant, trying to get him to choose a corner to dive to. Crane ran in and caught the ball more powerfully than you would have imagined. It fairly rocketed off his boot. Unfortunately, the ball had also been skied and flew way over the bar. He'd missed! If Dogs scored their next penalty, it would be back to level terms. Harry returned to the centre circle, head down, thoroughly dejected, but the boys and the staff consoled him as we waited for the next Wimbledogs player to step forward.

Ronnie Rottweiler had the chance to draw the teams level. He looked nervous as he approached the penalty spot. He only took a few steps for his run up, standing up on his back legs. He almost hopped forward before swinging his left boot at the ball. He scuffed his shot badly, kicking as much of the ground as the ball. The mis-kick had actually wrong-footed Jim, who had probably guessed the way it was meant to go. He'd dived to his right, but the ball had been scuffed so badly that it had ended up going towards the opposite corner. Time seemed to be frozen as the ball slowly rolled towards the goal. Jim was desperately trying to get up and over to the other side. He sprinted and dived full-stretch but the ball just had enough pace to beat him. Rottweiler breathed a dog's breath of relief. It had been very lucky, but it had gone in. We were three all, with four penalties taken each. This was going to the wire!

Young Bunny Sears was the fifth of the selected penalty takers. One more penalty each and then, if the scores were still level, we'd move onto sudden death. There was huge pressure on the young rabbit's shoulders. Some of us turned away, unable to watch. I was one of them. I didn't see the penalty until later on the T.V, but I could hear that the cheers had come from our supporters. Bunny had actually thumped the ball confidently into the top right-hand corner. Pheasant had no chance. 4-3!

The Dog's notorious captain, Vinnie Bones was the next penalty taker. He had to score. Boos and jeers came from our fans, as the pantomime villain approached the penalty spot.

He looked confident. He stood up on his hind legs and pushed out his chest, taking a deep breath before starting his run-up. He approached the ball and BANG; he'd thumped the ball hard and true towards the top right-hand corner. Under so much pressure, he'd taken a cracking penalty; unstoppable! But... nobody had told our Jim. With an incredible feat of athleticism, he sprang up into the top corner and got the very tips of his gloves onto the ball, tipping it onto the cross bar and away back towards Bones, who thumped the ball angrily into the sky. Our players and staff went into hysterics, as we chased down the pitch to celebrate with Jim. The fans went wild. We'd done it. We'd done it! WE'D DONE IT! Holding Jim aloft, we went to celebrate with our fans.

"Jim Pan Zee! Jim Pan Zee! Jim Pan Zee! Jim Pan Zee!"

Gazzer Grassnake and Jonjo Shellby
PODCAST

GG: Good evening and welcome to our latest podcast.

JS: Good evening, and what a time to be a Foalchester fan!

GG: You can say that again JS.

JS: Good evening, and what a time to be a Foalchester fan!

GG: Very funny JS!

JS: Thanks.

GG: So, what about that game against Wimbledogs? What drama!

JS: Incredible GG. I have to admit that when the penalties were being taken, I spent most of my time with my head in my shell. I just couldn't bear the tension.

GG: I know what you mean, I thought I was going to burst!

JS: Yuk!

GG: But the boys did it! What a battle! And what composure for the penalties! Against, it has to be said, a very physical, often overly physical, Wimbledogs team.

JS: Not known for their finesse are they GG? Some of the tackles were shocking. Credit to the boys, especially the younger lads for refusing to be intimidated. Great spirit!

GG: And what about Jim Pan Zee, JS? What a story!

JS: After all his off-field problems, and lack of match practice. What a show of character!

GG: And that final save... extraordinary! I've watched it back about twenty times and I still don't know how he managed to stop it! A world-class save!

JS: Definitely. So pleased for the lad! It almost felt like the script had been written for him, what with the injury to Albert Ross.

GG: Yeah, I know what you mean. Shame for Rossy though, but I'm sure he's happy for Jim. I know they're great mates!

JS: On that note, I'm pleased to say that Ross's injury is not as bad as it first appeared, and it's hoped that he could be available for selection next weekend. Good news.

GG: Good news indeed. Now, we have some very special guests in tonight don't we JS?

JS: We certainly do.

GG: We're delighted to welcome a couple of the so-called WAGS (Wives and Girlfriends) of the team. Not a term I really like, but the papers seem to love it.

JS: So, we actually have one wife, and one girlfriend. Firstly, we have Lily Longneck, glamorous wife of our skipper, Jack; and Priti Pretty, soon to be Priti Flamingo, girlfriend of our flying wing-back, Flamingo. Welcome to the show ladies.

Priti and Lily: Thank you very much.

GG: If I may, I'd like to start with you, Lily. Obviously, Jack has been in the game some time, and is the only one of the team to have played professional football, but how is he taking this incredible cup run?

LILY: Well, when he retired from professional football, the idea was to retire while he was still at the top of his game and just play a bit of non-league football for fun. Now he's playing in some of the biggest games of his career. He's never been in a team that's got past the last 16 of the F.A Cup before, so it's incredible that he's now going to be playing in a semi-final. He's loving it.

GG: Great! And I know that the other players really look up to him.

JS: Of course they look up to him, he's about 18 feet tall!

GG: Thank you, JS. I think Lily knows what I mean. The younger players, in particular, clearly see him as a positive role model.

LILY: Yes, well he loves to pass on his knowledge and experience and he's thoroughly enjoying his role. I know that he wants to move into coaching at some stage, so this is all valuable experience for him.

GG: Who knows, he may be coaching at Foalchester, or even become manager, in the future.

LILLY: Maybe at some stage, yes, but for now he's happy playing under Horsé. What a job *he's* doing!

GG: What a job indeed!

JS: Lily, if I might just ask you a couple of questions before we have a chat with Priti.

LILLY: Of course.

JS: Well, as most people are aware, you, yourself are quite a celebrity in your own right, as both a model and now more recently a fashion designer. I just wondered if you've had any advice for some of the other WAGS who are less used to being in the public eye.

LILY: Oh, yes, I know exactly how intrusive it can be, and how overwhelming, so, yes, I've tried to help the girls, and of course, Zebrado's boyfriend Zeb, who's got a lot of interest from the press.

JS: Yes, they've certainly latched onto Zebrado and Zeb, they're both quite flamboyant characters.

LILY: They're great! To be honest, I think Zeb's in his element with all the media coverage. He's something of an entertainer.

JS: It makes me laugh that they refer to him as one of the WAGS, I suppose Wives and girlfriends and boyfriends wouldn't really work as an acronym!

GG: Oooh, hark at you and your 'acronyms'! Are you trying to impress the ladies?

JS: Just sharing a bit of my extraordinary knowledge. Anyway, just a couple more questions. Firstly, you're immaculately dressed, do you have a favourite designer?

LILY: Apart from myself you mean (she laughs). I don't have a specific favourite, but I do like a lot of the designs by Giraffe Lauren. The dress I'm wearing now is a Giraffe Lauren actually.

JS: And you look amazing in it, if I may say so.

LILY: Thank you.

GG: Erm, JS, perhaps you could just wipe the side of your mouth; you're drooling.

JS: Just complimenting the lady.

GG: Really?

JS: Yes. Now just one final question, and this one's from my wife. She wants to know if your wonderful eyelashes are your own or fake? Sorry if that sounds a bit rude, she can be a little blunt.

LILY: (Laughing) That's fine. I've been asked that question before. They are all mine; very real. Us giraffes are very fortunate to have such naturally long lashes, in fact I hardly ever wear mascara.

JS: My wife is quite obsessed with your eyelashes. A few weeks ago, she found an area of wall that had been painted black. The paint was still wet, so she pushed one side of her face to the wall, and then the other, trying to create her own set of eyelashes.

LILY: And did it work?

JS: No. No, not really, she looked ridiculous. Who's ever heard of a snail with eyelashes? Honestly! After they'd smudged it looked like she had two black eyes. Of course, I didn't say anything...

GG: Erm, JS, you do realise that this is a live podcast, don't you?

JS: What...? oh... yes ... I'd forgotten... Oh.

GG: Oh indeed, I have a feeling there might be another pair of black eyes tonight Shelly me old mate. Anyway, it's time to have a quick chat with our other guest, Priti, soon to be Mrs Priti Flamingo. So, Priti, I guess my first question has to be, when is the big day?

PRITI: August the 14th. Not long to go now.

GG: Excited?

PRITI: I will be. I'll be glad when everything's been organised, and hopefully the day goes smoothly.

GG: I'm sure it will. And how is Flamingo feeling about the whole thing?

PRITI: Oh, he's fine. He just carries on with his football and his work.

GG: Ah, yes, how is the restaurant doing?

PRITI: Yeah, it seems to be going very well. Flamingo doesn't do so much of the actual cooking these days; he's got a couple of excellent chefs to do a lot of the work now. It gives him more time for training and matches.

GG: He must be very busy. Do you actually get to see much of him?

PRITI: To be honest, not all that much at the moment, especially during this cup run. When he's not playing football, or working in the restaurant, he's busy with interviews and media work. I don't mind though; it's an exciting time and he needs to make the most of it. This is probably a once-in-a-lifetime opportunity.

JS: Priti, if I might chip in. Firstly, I must say that you certainly live up to your name. Priti by name, and pretty by nature.

PRITI: Thank you.

GG: Don't you think you're in enough trouble with the wife, without flirting with all the guests?

JS: Just being friendly. Anyway, Priti, if I might ask a couple of questions.

PRITI: Certainly.

JS: Firstly, is it true that you are something of a sporty person yourself? I'm sure I've heard something about gymnastics.

PRITI: Yes, that's right, I still do a bit of gymnastics, but I also do some coaching now. I did compete for Great Britain when I was younger, specialising on the beam.

JS: You certainly have the body and the legs for it. All that natural standing on one leg must help with your balance.

GG: Flirting again JS?

PRITI: Yes, it is an advantage, I do have good natural balance.

JS: I'm sure. One more question, and this one comes again from my wife. How does it feel to have such long, slender legs?

PRITI: It's fine. It's just how I am. It's what flamingos are like.

JS: Yes, I know, it's a pretty silly question from a snail who is not meant to have legs, but she does have some strange thoughts at times. She never seems to be happy with how she is. It wouldn't surprise me if I turned up at home and found her hobbling along on some stilts made from lolly sticks or something! (He shakes his head and sighs). Funny woman!

GG: Have you got a death wish or something JS? Are you working on getting a divorce?

JS: Of course not. I love my wife.

GG: Maybe you need to try thinking, before you talk. I wouldn't want to be in your shoes when you get home tonight.

JS: I don't wear shoes.

GG: Anyway... That's the end of tonight's podcast. A special thank you to Priti and Lily, and let's all keep our fingers crossed for the next cup draw. Up the U's!

JS: Up the U's. Goodnight.

CHAPTER 14 –
BALL NUMBER 6

"Will play... ball number 6, Manechester United."

A huge roar went out around Pep's living room. Manechester United were the current champions of the Premier League and were one of the best teams in Europe. They'd also been the club I'd supported since I was 7 years old and living back home in Portugal with my football-mad parents. It was truly a dream come true. There was so much noise in the house that we didn't even hear the rest of the draw. We were bouncing! It was just what we needed after such a difficult few weeks. Manechester United at home. Manechester United coming to Foalchester. Manechester United at Mongoose Lane! Manechester United... I would have pinched myself to see if I was actually dreaming this or not, but it's not easy to pinch yourself when you've got hooves, so I just gave my head a quick shake. I wasn't dreaming. It was real. It was on the big screen. Foalchester United V Manechester United!!!

Between Pep and me, we had a huge decision to make. We were at home, and the game was also going to be live on T.V, but we only currently had a capacity of 800, hardly enough room for our own supporters, let alone Manechester United who had an enormous fan base. Pep told me that it would be possible to increase the capacity to just over 1500 by the time the match was played, but this was not really going to make a great deal of difference. We could, if we wished, talk to Manechester United about switching the match to their ground, Foal Stafford, with a capacity of over 85,000. In many ways this would make more sense but then we'd be giving away our home advantage and some of the local fans might struggle to make their way right up to Manechester. We decided to make a list of all the pros and cons involved and try to make a decision. Even then, we found the pros and cons were very closely balanced. The cup run, with the T.V money in particular, had yielded significant revenue so Pep proposed that we hire as many coaches as possible for the journey up to Manechester and to only charge the fans a very minimal fee. The balance would be paid for by the club. He also proposed that we should set up a big screen at our Mongoose Road ground so that any fans unable to make the journey could watch it free of charge, and with all facilities available. That clinched it. We were going to Foal Stafford!

I can still remember the players' faces when we told them what we proposed to do. Every single one of them was buzzing at the prospect of playing at one of the biggest and most famous grounds in Europe. I don't think any of them had even considered that we could possibly switch the venue, and they knew that this was likely to be a once-in-a-lifetime chance. The buzz around the group, staff included, was electric!

For a while at least, The Daily Lion, ceased knocking the club and players, and focused again on the football. Jonjo and Gazzer were swamped with media interest and had even received an invitation to appear alongside Gary Lionaker in the studio on the day of the game. Newspaper and internet articles focused largely on the players, their part time jobs, their previous footballing experiences and their individual personalities. There was also a noticeable build-up of interest in their partners and families (including mine). While it stayed friendly and only mildly intrusive, we, as a club, were happy enough to work alongside the media, but we were always aware that they could turn at any time, just like The Daily Lion.

The day arrived. We had been allocated 3000 tickets for the game and the vast majority of the fans had decided to travel on the coaches subsidised by the club (most birds were going to fly up). In all, there were 86 coaches, holding an average of about 30 fans each (you can do the Maths!). Some would be able to hold just 5 or six elephants, whilst others would hold 70 to 80 rabbits, and so on. As they congregated outside the ground at 8 a.m, it just looked like a massive wave of blue and white. We'd sold so much merchandise in the past few weeks and the fans were kitted out in scarfs, hats, replica kits (some with their favourite player's name printed on the back). I noticed that there was a whole group of fans with Horsés Heroes printed across the backs of their shirts. An ostrich had had all her feathers sprayed in blue and white stripes (it must have taken ages!). A lot of young monkey fans had had their faces painted blue and white, some with matching wigs. Several zebras had changed their black and white stripes to blue and white; a group of rattle snakes had tied additional Foalchester United blue and white rattles to their tails and a porcupine had had every spine meticulously coated in blue and white nail varnish. It was wonderful to see, and they also brought with them a fun, party atmosphere. I felt humbled just to be a part of it!

Pep had also arranged a separate, luxury coach for the WAGS to travel up to the game. Players without partners, such as young Jim Pan Zee, could bring along a family member or friend. Jack Longneck invited his elegant wife, Lily; Rhinaldo invited his girlfriend, Rhinata; Rhinodinio invited his girlfriend, Rhonda; Chi Tah invited his girlfriend, Tara; Jim Pan Zee invited his dad, Tim; Camelino invited his wife, Camilla; Lionelli invited his wife, Lionessie; Terry Trotter invited his wife, Sowsy (babysitters employed for the lively litter!), Harry Crane invited his wife, Jane; Flamingo invited his fiancé, Priti; Kenny Dogleash invited his wife, Penny; Moo Salah invited his fiancé, Moosa; Zebrado brought his

Camelino

Weight: 800 Kg
Speed: 35 MPH
Height: 1.8 M
Nickname: Humpy or Humpty

Favourite holiday destination:
Anywhere hot and sunny, e.g. desert.

Job:
Warehouse worker (mainly humping stuff about!)

Favourite singer:
Engelbert Humpydink (I don't really like much of the modern music!)

Favourite joke:
What do you call a camel in the Arctic?
Lost!

flamboyant boyfriend, Zeb; Marcus Ratface invited his girlfriend, Gerbilia; Biffy Biffendale-Chops invited his mother, Bertrude; Bunny Sears invited his sister, Lop; Albert Ross invited his brother, Jonathon; Ian Brush invited his wife, Cher, and Adam Allama invited his girlfriend, Alana. Pep's wife, Anna, and my wife, Mare-ria had chosen not to travel with us and were going to a health spa for the day instead. Jonjo Shellby's wife, Shelly, and Gazzer Grassnake's girlfriend, Susssan, were accompanying their partners to the BBC studios in central Manechester where Gazzer and Jonjo were to appear on Match of the Day.

Inside the changing room, there was an electric-like buzz of anticipation. Fifteen minutes until kick off! We could hear the noise of the crowd clearly; both sets of supporters in full voice. I'd kept the side very similar to the one that had done so well against Wimbledogs in the previous round, just bringing in Lionelli – who had now served his suspension – for Rhinodinio, and keeping Jim Pan Zee in goal for the not yet fully fit Albert Ross, who started on the bench. We also kept to the same 3-5-2 formation. The rest of the squad were all on the bench, including Moo Salah who was still having problems with his calf and wasn't really fit to play. As we could name up to eight substitutes, we gave him the opportunity to be involved in this once-in-a-lifetime match. All I said to the players was that they should enjoy the experience and play their own game. They didn't really need to be fired up for this one. They knew it was huge!

As Jack led the team onto the pitch, the cheers and applause rang out around the ground. One group of our fans were chanting my name. Pride swelled within me. It was truly incredible. On paper, they were much the superior side, with Sir Ibex Ferguson selecting a very strong side. Nine internationals in the starting eleven, including the England captain, Kanga Rooney. Amongst the other stars on show were, Lion Giggs, Nicky Buck, Doggy Charlton, David (the Emu) Peckem, Paul Foals, Bull Pogber, captain, Sty Keen, Paul Porker, and in goal, Cheetah Smikel. To our credit, they had not taken the risk of resting too many players, taking this match very seriously, and knowing that they were going to be in for a real match.

Jack won the toss and decided to kick off. The volume of the crowd went up another couple of notches. I hoped that some of the players, especially the younger ones, wouldn't be overawed by the magnitude of the occasion. Dogleash tapped the ball forward and Ratface played a simple pass back to Lionelli. We were off!

We played some nice, simple passes as we tried to settle into the game. We knew that Manechester would boss the possession, so we needed to make sure that when we had it, we retained it. Chi Tah then received the ball in midfield but was immediately closed down by the Manechester United skipper, Sty Keen. With trotters showing, Keen slid in and won the ball cleanly, then cleverly played a slide-rule pass onto the lively Rooney. Rooney bounded after the ball and hit an early shot before the Foalchester defenders could close him down. The shot flew off his boot, leaving Jim Pan Zee floundering hopelessly through the air. The ball though, thumped against the crossbar and rebounded back into the box, where Jack Longneck was able to clear the ball away from danger. An early let off.

On 14 minutes, a foul on Bull Pogber by Lionelli, gave David Peckem the chance to try one of his trademark freekicks. It was roughly five metres outside the box, just the sort of distance that he loved. It gave him the chance to get real bend and dip on the ball. Jim Pan Zee asked for a five-man wall, protecting the left-hand side of the goal. Peckem took a short run up and hit a wicked, bending and swerving shot over the wall, dipping into the top left-hand corner of the goal. Jim was rooted to the spot. It was a sweet strike and looked for all the world as though it was going to ripple into the back of the net. For the second time in the match though, the woodwork came to our rescue, as the still-bending ball, ricocheted off the inside of the upright and bounced across the goal line and into the grateful arms of Jim Pan Zee. Another lucky escape! We'd need more of these if we were ever going to win this game, but maybe... well just maybe, the Footballing Gods were with us.

On 20 minutes we had our first real foray into the opposition half, with Chi Tah bursting forward down the right, the ball seemingly stuck to his feet. As he reached the byline, and looked up to put in a cross, Lion Giggs sprang out of nowhere and blocked the ball. It was a corner. The first of the game for either side, and possibly our best chance of sneaking a goal. Harry Crane carefully placed the ball into the corner area and held his wings aloft, a message to the other players as to which routine we were going to try. Rhinaldo and Lionelli both made runs to the near post, but Crane curled in a ball towards the back post. Jack Longneck ran in from the edge of the six-yard box and comfortably got above his marker. He met the ball with enormous force and powered the ball into the back of the net. Cheetah Smikel had no chance! Completely against the run of play, we'd taken the lead! Captain Marvel had done it again! Our fans went wild, as the Manechester United fans watched on in disbelief. Foalchester United 1, Manechester United 0! All we had to do now was to hold on for another 70 minutes plus additional time (ALL we had to do!)

For the next ten minutes or so, Manechester United's players seemed to have been shell-shocked and made a number of uncustomary errors. For the first time in the game, we seemed relatively comfortable. I knew though, that a side like Manechester United, would inevitably get back on track and start to control the game again. We didn't dare take our foot off the pedal for a moment!

As I'd predicted, Manechester soon got their fluency back and were starting to apply more and more pressure.

On 35 minutes, Doggy Charlton crashed a shot at goal from a good 35 yards. He'd struck it cleanly, and it flew towards the top right of the goal. With extraordinary agility and speed, Jim Pan Zee pounced across the goal and tipped the ball over the bar. A truly incredible save! It remained 1 – 0 to us. Just. From the resulting corner, Kanga Rooney jumped up with both feet and hit a sweet volley from the edge of the box, only to see his goal-bound shot hit the back of his own player's head, David Peckham, and deflect harmlessly over the bar. Foalchester were living a charmed life. Could it last?

For the remaining ten minutes plus four minutes of additional time, the pressure continued but with almost all the Foalchester players behind the ball, Manechester United couldn't forge another clear goalscoring opportunity. Half time. A long half. Another even longer half to come. Could we? Could we? It was a massive ask.

Match of the Day studio

Gary Lionaker:	Well, Gazzer, Jonjo, what a half?
GG:	Just a bit Gary. The boys have done great! I can hardly believe it.
JS:	Can we stop the game now please? (Laughs)
Gary Lionaker:	If only Jonjo. Let's talk about the goal first, Jack Longneck, what a header! Great ball in from Craney too by the way.
GG:	What a player he is Gary. That was so typical of the big man. Yes, he's got the height, but it's the power and accuracy that he gets that's so impressive. Great ball in from Craney too as you say.
Gary Lionaker:	Very much so. Since the goal, it's certainly been backs to the wall, but what brave defending and some top saves from Jim Pan Zee.

Harry Crane

Weight: 4.5 Kg

Speed: 20 MPH (Not flying speed!)

Height: 125 cm

Favourite actor: Michael Crane

Favourite position:

Wing back/Winger

Nickname: Craney or Crazy Legs

Job: Crane Operator/Driver

Favourite joke:
What is a crane's
favourite drink?
Crane-berry juice!

JS: We're not going to leave anything behind, Gary, it's bodies on the line time and so far, we've managed to keep them out. Jim's been great too as you've said.

GG: The cross bar and post have also had a fantastic first half! (Laughs)

Gary Lionaker: (laughing) Have you had a ball magnet attached to the woodwork?

GG: That would be telling!

Gary Lionaker: Can you keep it going? That's the big question.

JS: Big ask Gary, but all I know is that the boys will give it their all. Yes, we're gonna need a huge chunk of luck but who knows? The romance of the cup...

Gary Lionaker: The romance of the cup indeed. You've certainly had a long love affair with it already. Can you take it all the way to the altar? I mean Wombat Stadium of course.

GG: Why not? Come on!!!

Gary Linaker: Thanks, Jonjo and Gazzer. Let's get back to the game and find out. I know how the neutrals want this to go. Oh, by the way, love the Podcast boys. Anyway, back to the action.

The changing room was buzzing as the boys came in. What a half! Yes, we'd clearly been second best in the match, but the fact was that we had got to half-time a goal up. We'd need more luck no doubt in the second half, all the players could do was what they'd already been doing; giving 100%. There were no injuries so I could see no reason to change the side at this stage. Substitutes would be vital later on as players started to tire from all the hustling and chasing they were doing. Most of the running was without the ball.

The pressure came on immediately at the restart, with Manechester United determined to get back on terms. A long-range effort from Bull Pogber flew a whisker wide of Jim Pan Zee's left-hand post. We were struggling just to get a touch of the ball, with Manechester knocking the ball about quickly and probing for openings. Foals received the ball inside the centre circle and played a slide-rule pass through to Lion Giggs, who took it in his stride and dribbled skilfully around the on-rushing Jim Pan Zee. Chi Tah had followed the run and sprinted like lightning to get back on the line, but Giggs cleverly dummied to shoot, sending Chi Tah sliding into the goal, before cooly side-footing the ball into the back of the net. It was 1 – 1, and we were only five minutes into the second half.

Buoyed on by their goal, Manechester United upped the pace once again, and we found ourselves almost completely encamped in our own half. I decided that we needed another player helping out defensively, so I substituted Kenny Dogleash, who as usual had run himself into the ground, despite having almost no service up front. He'd actually spent most of his time tracking back and making tackles in his own half. I brought on Eric Elephantona to add a bit of weight and power as a defensive midfielder, just in front of the back three, leaving just Marcus Ratface alone up front.

For the next 15 minutes, the change seemed to work as Manechester United, still playing some neat, quick football, failed to create a clear-cut chance. We were in no hurry when it came to our throw-ins or free-kicks, not time-wasting, just giving ourselves a bit of a breather; a much-needed breather. On 68 minutes, Terry Trotter tripped Doggy Charlton just outside the area. A free-kick in a dangerous position. Giggs and Rooney stood behind the ball. The position possibly favoured the left foot of Giggs, but it was Rooney who curled the shot around the wall. Jim Pan Zee made a desperate dive to his left, but the ball had been hit too cleanly for him to reach. The ball hit the inside of the post and bounced back towards Jim, now sprawled across the ground. It hit him on the top of his head and bounced back into the post again, before finally rolling back within his grasp. With great relief, and before on-rushing United players could scramble the ball over the line, Jim threw himself on top of the ball and brought it into his body. Another amazing let-off. At this rate, the woodwork was going to be voted as our player of the match!

On 75 minutes, I made two more substitutions, bringing Adam Allama on for Rhinaldo, and Bunny Sears on for Marcus Ratface. There was no real tactical reason for this, just a need for some fresh legs on the pitch. The clock kept ticking, and we entered the 86th minute. Paul Porker made a fabulous run down the right and whipped in a delightful ball. For once, the Foalchester defence had not been able to get properly positioned and the ball picked out an unmarked Bull Pogber, just outside the six-yard box. Jim Pan Zee had come for the cross but had got nowhere near it. It was a free header. He had to score! But, inexplicably, Pogber somehow managed to completely misjudge the header and it just skimmed off his head and went harmlessly wide. A dreadful miss! A real sitter! In the technical area, I gave a huge sigh of relief. Somehow, we were still level. Four minutes plus whatever the ref decided to add on to go, until we went into 30 minutes of extra time. What an achievement that would be!

Then – the extraordinary happened! Elephantona met a cross with a thumping clearance and the ball flew into the United half. United had pushed so far forwards that Bunny Sears suddenly found himself one-on-one at the back. Sears nutmegged Nicky Buck and was running towards goal. Could this be the moment? Could he...? Sty Keen was desperately trying to make up the ground, but Sears pace kept him half a yard ahead. He was just outside the area and now needed to make a decision, whether to take a shot early or wait for the keeper to make his move. Clearly in two minds, Sears tripped over his own feet on the edge of the box. Keen slid in and put the ball out for a corner. The chance had gone. Bunny Sears held his head in his paws, he knew that he'd just had the chance to make history. Then he noticed that the referee's assistant, Graham Mole, had his flag up. Sears was partly relieved that he'd been flagged offside as it wouldn't have counted even if he had finished the chance. Meanwhile, the referee had made his way over to Graham Mole on the touchline. Then, incredibly, he blew his whistle and pointed at the spot! But that wasn't the end of it. He called Keen over and showed him a straight red card! Everyone in the crowd seemed shocked. All the players were shrugging shoulders and looking confused. Sears was speaking to the ref and shaking his head. The Manechester United players were both fuming, and stunned. Keen had to be escorted off the pitch by two of the United substitutes. Ibex Ferguson was trotting up and down his technical area looking as though he might explode any minute. It was chaos!

As all this was going on, I called our players over and we formed a huddle on the touchline. Then, finally, the whistle blew, and our penalty taker was called over. With Rhinaldo (our usual penalty taker) off the pitch, Jack Longneck had taken on the responsibility. As cool and classy as always, he made his way towards the spot and used his long neck to set the ball correctly. He then took a moment, looked over towards all of his teammates and the staff on the sidelines before beginning his run up. He strode forward with purpose, looking as though he was going to go for sheer power, but then, at the last moment he slowed and deliberately rolled the ball slowly forward with his hoof, straight towards Cheetah Smikel. Smikel had actually dived early to his right but still had plenty of time to get himself back up and pick up the ball. Jack looked at him and gave a slow meaningful bow, then returned to his position. Applause slowly began to ripple around the ground as they started to realise what had happened.

The match continued, United down to ten men. Then Paul Foals received the ball just outside the area. The 90 minutes were up and there had been three minutes added. Foals, with hardly any back lift, and little room to work in, unleashed a fantastic shot that flew into the bottom left-hand corner. Jim Pan Zee hadn't even seen it. 2 – 1 to Manechester United and just seconds left. From the kick-off, Sears tried a speculative shot that had the accuracy, but not the power, to trouble Smikel. He picked up the ball, bounced it a couple of times and then launched it forward. The whistle went. The match was over. The amazing cup run had come to an even more amazing end.

Both teams were applauded off the pitch, both sets of fans applauding both teams. A remarkable match, a remarkable occasion and, well, just remarkable!!

Match of the Day studio

Gary Lionaker:	I'm lost for words. I am genuinely lost for words.
GG:	*You* are?
JS:	I think everyone is.
Gary Lionaker:	What just happened? Did it just happen?
JS:	It's real Gary...
Gary Lionaker:	I've certainly seen some things in football before, and in sport in general. Incredible things, shocking things, brilliant things, but I don't think I've ever seen such an extraordinary show of sportsmanship. A massive chance to possibly win the game. But then... well... staggered...!
GG:	I think it just shows what a group of players and staff, we've got at our club.

Gary Lionaker: Would Horsé have made that decision? Was that what the huddle was about do you think? Or did Jack just take it upon himself?

JS: Knowing them as we do, and knowing Horsé and Jack, I'm sure that it would have been a whole team decision.

Gary Lionaker: So, everyone agreed... even knowing what was at stake?

JS: I'm almost certain, that's what would have happened.

Gary Lionaker: Extraordinary. I must just ask, how do you two feel?

JS and GG: (They look at each other before answering) Proud. Just very, very proud!

Gary Lionaker: No regrets?

JS: No. We'd all have loved to have won the tie, but, at the end of the day, it was never a penalty, not in a million years. The referee's assistant must have been the only person on the whole planet who hadn't seen, firstly that Bunny had tripped over his own feet, and secondly that he was clearly outside the area anyway.

Gary Lionaker: It certainly was a dreadful decision. I guess the referee couldn't tell from where he was positioned. But the assistant was in a great position.

GG: I know we have to be careful what we say about the officials, but we have come across Mr Mole before. That time it worked against us. Perhaps that's what clinched our decision to miss the penalty, knowing how it feels when decisions have been wrongly made against you.

Gary Lionaker: I guess it also begs the question of why VAR wasn't used in today's game.

GG: Quite possibly Gary, it was a big game and it's been marred by one 'clear and obvious' error.

Gary Lionaker: I'm not a big VAR fan, but on this occasion...? Anyway, gentlemen, thanks for coming in and giving us your thoughts, it's been a real pleasure. What an incredible day, in the incredible, and unpredictable world of F.A Cup football!

NEWSPAPER HEADLINES

Horsés Heroes – Daily Snail

Horsés Heroes – The Mirror Carp

Horsés Heroes – The Telegiraffe

Heroes or fools? – The Daily Lion

Bison Fury wins I'm a Celebrity Get Me Out of Here – The Starfish

Horsés Heroes – Foalchester Gazette

CHAPTER 15 –
THEY THINK IT'S ALL OVER...

So that was it. The cup run, glorious as it had been, was finally over. We'd certainly won many plaudits and received massive praise for our sporting actions, but the cup was over, for this year at least. We had three league games to go and then the season was finished. We were currently lying in 7th place in the league, with just an outside chance of making the playoffs. The media interest in the club and its players and staff was quite extraordinary. The country, it seemed, still wanted more. We'd been the great underdogs, the people's heroes, but there was still a huge thirst for more information, for more insights, more stories. Every single player and member of staff had become celebrities in their own right. There were TV interviews, radio interviews, offers to appear on TV reality shows, and even the mention of a film based on our exploits.

Despite all this, however, there was still a slight, but noticeable, feeling of anti-climax. None of us regretted our decision to deliberately miss the penalty, but we also realised that it was unlikely that we'd ever have such an opportunity to play at Wombat Stadium ever again. We felt it mostly for Jack, who had already announced that he would be retiring from football as a player, having already agreed to work as Head Coach at Championship side, Blackbird Rovers.

But then....

Six weeks later, with the season now finished (we won two and lost one of the remaining matches – finishing the season in 7th place), a letter arrived at the club. That wasn't so surprising, we'd received literally thousands of letters, but this one was different. Even the envelope looked different. Pep was with me in the office at the time, finishing off some paperwork. I showed him the envelope, and we both noticed the special seal on it. He looked at me and then nodded for me to open it. Luckily, I was sitting down, or else there may well have been a half tonne of horse flesh lying on the floor. It was from the Palace. No, not Crystal Palace, THE PALACE. It was a letter, direct from the King. In fact, it was an invitation.

He'd been following our exploits with great interest and had been 'bowled over' (his words, not mine) by our adventure, and especially our remarkable sense of fair play and sportsmanship. He had personally asked his people if they could arrange a special match for us, to celebrate the way that we had conducted ourselves, and especially the 'monumental' decision we'd made in the semi-final against Manechester United. It had therefore been arranged that we were to play in a charity match (a charity of our choice), on the 15th of August, against an all-star Premier League team, at... wait for it... wait for it...Wombat Stadium! Attending the match itself would be King Charles the Spaniel, along with the Queen Consort, Chinchilla. Wombat Stadium!! Wombat Stadium!! In front of our King and Queen Consort!! Pep and I just stared at each other in disbelief. The dream was to continue for one more game.

EPILOGUE

- We lost the game 6 – 1. Every player and member of staff, including Gazzer and Jonjo, and Pep and myself, got some time on the pitch. I got an assist for Bunny Sears' goal! (Just thought I'd mention it!!)
- King Charles the Spaniel awarded all the players involved, a Golden medallion.
- We raised over £300,000 to be split between the charities: Offspring in Need and Victims of Crime (suggested by the Rhino twins).
- Pep, Jack Longneck and I were all awarded MBEs in the New Years Honours List.
- 'Horsés Heroes' – the film, has been commissioned and filming has already started.

In short, it was the most amazing, incredible, extraordinary and wonderful end to an amazing, incredible, extraordinary and wonderful year. And next year? Who knows...

THE FINAL WHISTLE!

Footnote: Anyone affected by Jim Pan Zee's battle with banana addiction can receive support from www.bananaddiction. co.uk or helpline 02476 141419 (Free Call)

www.ingramcontent.com/pod-product-compliance
Lightning Source LLC
Chambersburg PA
CBHW041605240626
47164CB00008B/179